LOCKED WORLDS

By
EDMOND HAMILTON

ARMCHAIR FICTION
PO Box 4369, Medford, Oregon 97504

For more information about Armchair Books and products, visit our website at…

www.armchairfiction.com

Or email us at…

armchairfiction@yahoo.com

WILL INSECTS RULE THE WORLD?

In a controversial experiment in physics, Dr. Adams set out to prove his wild theory that the atom was the key to an alternate world—a world that was tied to our own. Bombarded with criticism from his peers, he concocted a fantastic and diabolical plan to turn the world into a living hell. However, when two of his peers, Harker and Rawlins, discovered the truth about Adams and his plans, they raced against time to find a way to stop him from destroying not just one world, but two! However, they soon learned that the horror they faced together wasn't nearly as bad as the horror that would come to pass if Adams' insane plans weren't stopped.

This is a most unique and original story, penned by one of the true masters of science fiction, Edmond Hamilton. It fairly bristles with exploits in the fourth dimension and foreign worlds, laden with adventure and excitement throughout.

FOR A SECOND COMPLETE NOVEL, TURN TO PAGE 93

CAST OF CHARACTERS

HARKER
His whole world was about to become a nightmare, unless he could stop Adams and the spider-men—but he was running out of time!

DR. ADAMS
This dark, but brilliant physicist was not a popular man on campus and had grown hateful of his critics. He planned to teach them a lesson they would never forget.

RAWLINS
His job as assistant to Dr. Adams was ideal at first, but his respect for the great doctor waned as he watched him slowly slip into madness.

NOR-KAN
If you needed someone to help you escape from a tower prison, or plan an armed assault, Nor-Kan was definitely your man! Umm, Bird-man, that is…

THE SPIDER-MEN
These "men" were bred to be servants, with intelligence bred into them; and they had grown weary of their boring way of life in their very dull world.

CHAPTER ONE

IN giving this record to the world, it has not been my purpose to enter into the speculation and discussion aroused by some phases of it. Rather it has been my intention to present only my personal experience of the matter, from its first beginning with Dr. Adams' sensational theory to its mighty, world-shaking end. For these reasons, therefore, I have striven throughout to avoid all questions of controversy, and except for some facts, which were public knowledge at the time, have confined my account entirely to those things, which I either saw or did.

It is with Dr. Adams himself that I choose to begin. For more than a dozen years he had been the head of the Physics Department at Northeastern University, where I held my one humble instructorship in English, and where his work had raised him to the level of the very highest authorities in his chosen field of science. Though still on the best side of forty, his additions to atomic science had made his name known to physicists in laboratories and lecture-halls across half the world. He was; without doubt, the most noted figure at Northeastern, and was at the same time the least-liked.

Tall, dark and bitter, with black, probing eyes and a turn for satire that could cut like a whiplash, he was decidedly antagonistic to most people. Among us of the faculty, indeed, he had no close friends or intimates whatever, with the exception of young Rawlins, his instructor-assistant, who was a particular friend of my own and as much liked as his superior was disliked. I do not think, myself, that Rawlins had any more real, liking for Dr. Adams than any of us, but the physicist's great scientific attainments had ennobled him in the eyes of the younger man, who would never listen to anything we might say against his superior.

There was much that was said against him, indeed, since Adams' brusque manners and contemptuous indifference to his colleagues could not fail to rub some of us the wrong way. We frankly disliked him, and were not slow in expressing our dislike, yet at the same time, even among ourselves, we respected him. The man's utter, fierce devotion to his science would have won that respect from anyone, and it was heightened by the great work he had done and was doing. Much of that work, it was true, was so highly technical in nature that we could not understand it, for all Rawlins enthusiastic explanations, but we did comprehend that Adams was doing revolutionary things in the field of atomic structure.

He had followed in the steps of Thomson and Rutherford in his special study of the atom, that inconceivably minute particle of elemental matter which was once considered indivisible, but which we now know is composed of a varying number of electrons, or tiny negative charges of electricity, revolving about a central positive charge or charges, the nucleus. It is intensely delicate work, the most delicate, indeed, in all science, this study of the natures of atoms and the movements of electrons. For though they are never to be seen, in, their incredible smallness, by even the most powerful of man's microscopes, yet they may be studied and investigated through their effects upon larger and visible particles of matter.

In this work Adams had gone far, and was considered, as we all knew, as ranking with the greatest of the English and German physicists in his atomic and electronic investigations. He had been one of the first to suggest the possibility of discharging electrons in controlled streams, the so-called cathode rays. He had partly anticipated and duplicated the famous Rutherford experiments, in which actual transmutation of elements had been accomplished by taking electrons from the atomic structure. It seemed, indeed, that he was but rising to new heights of achievement and fame, when there came suddenly, darkening all that he had already done, the publication of his sensational "interlocking atom" theory.

It was late in April that we of the university first heard of Adams' new theory, through Rawlins, who had taken some part in the experiments leading up to it, and who was very enthusiastic concerning it. His lengthy and involved explanations of it were too technical for us, and I waved him aside in mock horror when he began them, but a few weeks later Adams' monograph concerning it was published, and the sensation which it aroused stirred in all us some interest in the thing. Partly by a reading of the monograph, whole sections of which were far too technical for my wits, and partly through Rawlins' eager accounts, I managed to get a fairly clear idea of the theory, which within a week or so of publication was kicking up a tempest in a teapot among all right-thinking physicists.

ADAMS prefaced the body of his monograph by stating that the main interest of his whole scientific career had lain in the study of atomic structure, and that he had now to present a new theory concerning that structure whose implications were revolutionary to certain accepted physical laws. He began by pointing out that the spaces between the revolving electrons of each atom are quite immense in proportion to their size. The planets that whirl about our sun, indeed, are not proportionately farther from each other than are the electrons of every atom. It was from a study of these spaces that Adams had brought forth his theory.

"During experiments of the last few months," he wrote, "I have been primarily concerned with a study of the motions and spacing of the revolving electrons of the atom, and have discovered a startling fact. You know that it has been suggested by scientists and by fiction writers that there might exist electronic systems, or atoms, wholly independent of the electronic systems which are our atoms, electronic systems which move through our electronic systems and form totally different atoms and worlds. This suggestion has been made many times, but without any basis of fact or truth, since we know that such electronic systems could not move through our own electronic systems without the nuclei of the one crashing into the nuclei of the other and destroying all, just as solar systems could not move through other solar systems without the suns of one crashing into the suns of the other and destroying both. Scientists have long known, though, that inside the electronic systems, which are our atoms, there exist what seem to be stray electrons, electrons that revolve in an opposite direction to our electrons, though about the same nuclei. For we have learned that just as the planets of our solar system all revolve about our Sun in the same direction, so in every atom of our world do the electrons revolve about their nucleus in the same direction, each one of our atoms being exactly like all the rest in the direction in which its electrons revolve about their nucleus. Yet in our atoms there exist, also, as I have said, these stray electrons, which do not belong to our own electronic systems, but revolve about the same nuclei in an opposite direction.

"Suppose that this were the case in our universe, suppose that beside the planets of our own solar system there were planets, which revolved about our sun in an opposite direction to our own. You see what that would mean? It would mean that in our one universe there would be two solar systems instead of one. Two solar systems moving about the same sun, but entirely apart and distinct from each other, two solar systems locked together in the space of one planetary universe, moving about the same sun, yet totally different from each other by reason of their opposite motions. And it is the same; I have found, in the atoms, the electronic systems, of our world, our universe. For these electrons, which we have considered stray electrons, and which move about the same nuclei as ours but in an opposite direction, form electronic systems totally different from our own. They are locked in the same space and move about the same nuclei, form atoms locked within our atoms and unknown and unseen to us, form worlds locked within our worlds. Unknown to and unseen by us, those worlds, those atoms, for though locked within our own worlds and atoms they seem to us only stray electrons, infinitely tiny electrical charges, moving opposite to our own electronic systems. While to those other atoms, to a dweller in the world locked in ours, our world in turn would seem only stray electrons moving opposite to *their* electronic systems. Just as if, were two opposite-moving solar systems locked together about the same sun as I have suggested, each would seem to the other only a few stray planets moving through their own system, neither system guessing or dreaming that an equally real and concrete system was locked within itself.

"Thus have we two worlds, our own and that interlocking one, the atoms of each one locked within the atoms of the other, their electrons moving in opposite directions about the same nuclei, yet neither world dreaming of the existence of the other. And an atom of one kind in one world might be interlocked with an atom of a totally different kind in the other, though their nuclei were one and the same. Two electrons revolving about their nucleus in one direction might form an atom of helium in this world, whereas if but one electron revolved about the same nucleus in the opposite direction, it would form in the interlocking world not an atom of helium but an atom of hydrogen. Thus we might have two totally different worlds, two universes, locked together atom within atom, and yet separated from each other by a gulf proportionately greater than that between the stars by the fact that though their electrons revolve about the same nuclei, they revolve in opposite directions.

"But suppose you take the helium atom in this world, with its two revolving electrons, and with one electron revolving in the opposite direction to form a hydrogen atom in the interlocking world, and suppose you reverse the motions of both electronic systems at the same moment, setting the two electrons revolving in the former direction of the one, and the one in the former direction of the two. If you were merely to halt the motions of the electrons you would only annihilate both atoms instantly, but if you were to reverse them as I have suggested, then you would have changed the two-electron atom of helium in this world into a one-electron atom of hydrogen, and at the same time would have changed the corresponding one-electron atom of hydrogen in the interlocking world into a two electron atom of helium. In other words, you would have transposed your atom of helium in this world into the interlocking world, and would have transposed the corresponding atom of hydrogen in that world into this one. If men can control the motions of electrons as they have done in the cathode rays and in the transmutation of elements, there is no reason why they cannot sometime control them so as to be able to accomplish this reversal of electronic motions. And when they can do so, they will be able to transpose any atom, any matter that atoms make up, from this world in the interlocking one, and the corresponding matter of that world into this one, and can enter that world at will."

These were the most significant paragraphs in Adams first statement of his theory, and, reading them, one hardly surprised by the criticism which they called forth, criticism of a bitterness almost unprecedented in the realms of scientific discussion. That bitterness, I think, was intensified by the contemptuous indifference with which Adams had always treated the majority of his fellow physicists, and which had made for him a host of enemies. Even without those enemies, so radical a theory as his would have met with a rough reception no doubt, but when the critics of that theory were almost unanimous in disliking the man who had propounded it, it is not astonishing that their opinions of it were of an unusually cutting nature.

The idea of the interlocking of atoms, of two wholly; different electronic systems moving in opposite directions about the same nucleus, was assailed and derided on all sides, only a few unimportant physicists here and there admitted that it might be possible. The great majority of Adams' fellow-scientists, to their own discredit, did not refute or attack his propositions by data of their own or by logical objections, but instead simply asked whether any sane person could believe that two atoms or electronic systems could interlock with each other about the same nucleus, or that two masses of concrete matter, two worlds, could exist in the same space at the same time, yet each wholly invisible to and unsuspected by the other. They admitted that Adams' account of the loose or stray electrons discovered moving through the spaces between the electrons of our own atomic structures was correct, but denied that these formed any electronic system of their own, since, as they pointed out, their motions and existence had already been plausibly explained in a score of different ways. They concluded their attacks, for the most part, by demanding that Adams bring forward the experimental proof of his theory, which he had mentioned in his monograph.

I THINK now that in the case of a lesser man, the whole theory would only have been contemptuously dismissed, rather than attacked with such force. It was too good a chance against the satiric and arrogant Adams for his enemies to miss, and instead of dropping the matter after their first attacks they continued to press him for proof or for retraction of his theory. Adams himself seemed to pay no attention whatever to his critics, deigning, no reply to them, but there was a set look in his face and a growing fierceness in his eyes that boded ill, I cannot deny that among the rest of us at the university there was no little satisfaction in seeing the sarcastic physicist thus humbled, though we all felt that the process was being carried a little too far. But Rawlins was still on the side of his superior, and was of the belief that in time the latter would vindicate his theory with irrefutable evidence.

"He's given up everything else, and is working late each night with these atomic structure experiments," Rawlins told me, as we lounged with our pipes one evening in my rooms. "He's going on with the same work that led up to his theory, and though he won't let me in with him now, I think that he'll succeed yet, and prove the whole thing up to the hilt."

"Prove fiddlesticks," I retorted unbelievingly. "He must be as insane as his own theory to try to find proof for it."

Rawlins shook his head, "I don't know. The theory seems a wild one, of course, but Adams is not the kind to go off half-cocked, and the extra-electronic motions, his theory's built on do exist—I went far enough with him in his experiments to know that."

I laughed. "It would take more than a few extra electrons zipping between our own to make me believe that solid matter can interlock with solid matter, world with world," I told him.

The greater number of those at the university, whatever their scientific attainments, were of my opinion, and it became evident that, beneath their disapproval and the unceasing criticism from without, Adams' position was becoming daily more uncomfortable. We heard, in a roundabout way, that the university's venerable president had paid a friendly call upon Adams and had urged him to clear up the whole business and prevent the university's name from being lowered by an undignified academic brawl, by presenting his proof, if he had any, or by retracting his statements. To this suggestion, as we learned later, Adams had replied in vitriolic terms, stating calmly that it was not his custom to spend his time convincing idiots of what he himself knew to be true, and that the agitation and controversy of the scientific world over his statements did not concern him in the least. He also added, for the benefit of the president, that he was but little concerned with the good or bad name of the university, since he counted himself a scientist and scholar rather than an academic politician.

Any lesser man, speaking thus, would have insured his own instant dismissal, and we expected momentarily to hear of Adams' dismissal. The whole matter, indeed, seemed to be rising into an open uproar, for the attacks upon the physicist had been increased and intensified by his own contemptuous silence. The thing could hardly be kept from breaking into an open row much longer, we knew, and we waited, with a certain zest, I must admit, for the opening of the battle. And then, with anti-climactic effect, Adams did the thing none of us had ever dreamed he would do. He shirked the coming battle and left the university.

It was between days that he left, unknown to and unseen by any in the whole institution, so far as could be learned,

Rawlins reported that he had worked late in his laboratory on the night before, so late, indeed, that none had been awake to see him leave the building. The lights he had left burning in the place, and a curious tangle of complicated apparatus was found there whose purpose none could fathom. There was a great disk of shining metal some ten feet in diameter, lying on the laboratory floor, with a similar great disk suspended some eight feet directly above it, the two being connected to a mass of strange-looking generators, coils and switches. On the disk on the floor was a round section or mass of a curious blue clay or soil, several inches deep, and which it was assumed that Adams had been testing. It seemed strange that he should have left the laboratory in such disorder, but a visit to his rooms had disclosed the fact that the same conditions prevailed there; only a few of his possessions were gone; the rest was carelessly left. It was the exit of a fugitive, of a coward, that he had made, we agreed, and the strange note, which he had left for the president, did not change our opinion.

That brief note, which was read to us at the next meeting of the faculty was so strange indeed as almost to hint the possibility of a disordered mind. It read:

I am leaving the university and my position in the world of men for reasons, which must be quite clear, to all. Having made one of the greatest additions to scientific knowledge ever made by man, I have found myself subjected to unceasing ridicule and criticism. The world, in the person of its so-called scientific men, has demanded that I either retract my theory or present proof of it, I cannot retract that which I know to be true, but I can and will present proof, proof which even this ignorant and incredulous world will be forced to accept; proof which, I venture to assert, this world and all upon it shall never to their end forget.

WITH the reading of that amazing note we all, I think, came to look on Adams as a self-deluded fakir who had fled with only one final burst of bravado. The note itself, of course, was never given to the public, but it was known that Adams had left the university secretly and without controversy, and that proved to the satisfaction of all that the physicist's pretensions had been demolished by the devastating criticism leveled against them. None of us knew where Adams might have gone, and not one of us, with the exception of Rawlins, was much interested in the question, Adams' incomprehensible masses of apparatus were cleared away, another man took his place as the department head, and within a few weeks all was as quiet and serene as before the publication of Adams' crazy theory.

It was all of a month after the sensation of it had subsided that Rawlins came to my rooms, one June evening, with a strange thoughtfulness apparent in his face and manner. He had taken to heart, more than any of us, the affair in which his superior had been implicated, but I had thought that he had put the matter from his mind since then, especially since he had not mentioned it to any of us. On this evening, however; after sitting silent for a time, smoking, he turned suddenly to me with a question.

"Harker, does it ever occur to you to wonder where Adams went?"

I looked sharply up at the question. "Why, no," I answered, with some surprise. "He left so strangely—I suppose he just went off somewhere to get clear of the whole affair."

"He left strangely, yes," said Rawlins. "But for where? All his belongings, almost, he left behind him. No one at all saw him go, and though I've made inquiries, he's never been heard from since that night!"

I was startled. "But he must have gone somewhere," I protested. "What are you getting at, Rawlins!"

My companion paused a moment before replying. "Harker," he finally said, "I knew Adams as well as anyone here, and though I had no personal liking for him, I know that he was not the type to run away from a battle. He was working day and night on his experiments through all that affair, working to get positive proof of his theory, to actually prove the existence of the interlocking world by transposing matter from this world to that, and from that to this. And if his experiments succeeded, as I believe they did, then he could well have performed the experiment on himself and transposed himself into that interlocking world."

"Good Lord, Rawlins!" I exclaimed. "You believe that? Believe that he was right about his interlocking world, and instead of leaving that night, transposed himself into that world!"

He nodded. "Yes. He went into the laboratory that night, Harker, but none ever saw him leave it. If he left it, he must have left it by that great disk-apparatus he had built, transposed himself by it into the world whose atoms interlock ours. I have studied that apparatus and I now firmly believe that it was built for that purpose, since it projects, from the upper disk to the lower, a ray similar to the radioactive rays used to break down atomic structures by Rutherford, a ray which halts the revolution of electrons in any matter on the lower disk and reverses their motions, causes them to revolve about their nuclei in the opposite direction, at the same time reversing the motions of the other electrons, the other electronic system, transposing the matter on the disk into the interlocking world, and the corresponding matter in that world into this one. You remember the mass of strange blue clay found on the disk? What was that, but the corresponding matter in the interlocking world, flashed into this one as the ray flashed Adams himself into that world!"

"It seems possible," I admitted, staggered by the idea, "yet the whole thing is so strange. Why should he want to go into that other world, even if he could? Why not call his critics together and show them the thing for proof?"

Rawlins shook his head. "He was a strange man, Harker, a monomaniac in some ways, I think. His anger against his critics, against the world that condemned him, was intense, for all his silence, and it was not justice that he wanted, but revenge. I think that he went into that interlocking world with his anger against our own world flaming high, determined, as he stated in his last note, to give it a proof, a terrible proof, that it would never forget. And I think that that proof, that terror, is hovering now above an unsuspecting world."

He reached into a pocket, drew forth a few newspaper clippings, and handed one to me. "This appeared in a New York paper over two weeks ago," he said, "I wonder if you will see in it the importance that I do."

I took the little article in my hand. It was not more than a few inches in length, apparently a brief cable dispatch.

"Paramaribo, Dutch Guiana, May 26. Officials of the trading post located here report that an intense excitement of some sort appears to be stirring the native tribes in the little-known region in the southern interior. The natives assert that a small hill lying a few miles from their principal village vanished suddenly a few nights ago in full view of all the village, without quake or disturbance of any kind, being replaced by a round patch of bluish soil. An intense panic has swept over all near-by tribes as a result of this story. It is believed at this place that the foundation of the tale is a landslide or earthquake of some sort, exaggerated by native superstition, though no such disturbances have been noticed here."

I raised my eyes to Rawlins', wonderingly. "I can't see the significance of that," I told him.

"Neither did I, at first," he said. "But read this one."

The second clipping he handed me was somewhat longer than the first, dated a few days later, and had evidently been written in a jocular vein by some humorous reporter. It read:

CAP'N JONAH OUTDONE BY MODERN MARINERS

First Mate and Operator of Steamship *Cherokee* Report Appearance of Floating Island

---

"New York, May 29. The age-old laurels of Captain Jonah as a teller of tall sea-tales are apparently in danger of being awarded to Robert Simms and E, Riley, First Mate and Radio Operator of the Blue Line freighter *Cherokee,* which arrived here from Hamburg yesterday morning.

"The two men in question are vehement in asserting the truth of their story, though their shipmates put it all down to the influence of the moonlight. It occurred, they say, on the night of the 27th, when the *Cherokee* was still several hundred miles east of New York. The mate was on the bridge, that night, and was joined shortly before midnight, he says, by the operator, Riley. They deny that any liquid refreshments were indulged in, and assert that they were both gazing over the moonlit sea when the thing happened.

"Both Simms and Riley are rather confused, unfortunately, as to just what did happen, but the kernel of their tale is that suddenly, in the sea a few hundred yards from the ship, a great circle of the waters seemed to vanish abruptly, without any unusual sound, to be replaced in the same instant by a great circle of solid ground of the same size, which hovered on the waters for a moment like a floating island and then sank from sight. It all happened so quickly, they assert, that they had no time to call any of their shipmates.

"Neither of the two men profess to know from where the island appeared so quickly and quietly, and as they assert that it was not there a moment before, it could only have been a submersible island coming up for a breath of air. As the remainder of the crew saw nothing of it, however, it is likely that the instantaneous island will be ignored by the geographers. When asked for his opinion on it, Captain Martin Cappen, master of the *Cherokee,* replied, 'The only thing of which I am convinced is that the liquor sold in Hamburg is of a very high power.' With Captain Cappen's opinion, the unbelieving world at large will very probably agree."

I looked up from that clipping with the strange idea of what Rawlins was driving at dawning across my mind. Silently I took the last one, which he held out, and hastily scanned it. It was as brief as the first one, an inch-long press-note from a small Iowa town.

"Gorland, Iowa, May 29. J. N. Lurkan, a farmer residing some six miles south of this community, has reported an odd change in soil, which has attracted some attention in this section. He states that a day ago he discovered that a section of pastureland on his farm, acres in extent, had changed overnight from close-cropped pasture to a barren blue clay unlike any ever seen in this section. The section of ground affected was in the shape of a great circle, apparently, and as it is a little lower in level than the surrounding ground, it is his opinion that a washout of some kind must have stripped away the ground from above. Neighbors, however, say that this is impossible since there have been no heavy rains in that district for the last few weeks."

I laid down that clipping and Rawlins and I stared at each other silently, intently. My brain was spinning with the thing that had suggested itself from a reading of those three clippings, a thing too stupendous and undreamed-of ever to happen, it seemed, and yet one that apparently had happened. At last the voice of Rawlins broke the silence.

"You see the similarity of these three happenings, Harker? In each case a circle of familiar matter was whiffed away and replaced by one of unfamiliar matter, the hill, the circle of ocean, and the circle of farmland, the first and the last being replaced, as you see, by a strange blue clay, a strange blue clay which we too found—there on the disk in the laboratory. And that can mean but one thing—can mean only that Adams transposed himself into that interlocking world and now, using the same principle, has transposed great sections of our world into that one, from Guiana and the Atlantic and Iowa."

"But why?" I asked, and his face grew grave.

"I think that I can guess why," he said, slowly. "Adams went into that world mad for vengeance upon this one, and now he is able, apparently, to transpose great sections of matter from world to world at will. I think that these first transpositions are but tests, and that since they have been successful the hour of his vengeance is at hand. And that vengeance—what will it be? Cities and millions of humans whirled into that world by his power, replaced here on earth by the barren clay of that world? Seas of that world, maybe, transposed to this one and released to drown humanity? Strange beasts, strange beings, sent into our world to destroy, and kill?"

I shrank from that awful vision. "But what can we do?" I cried, and then Rawlins' eyes gleamed with purpose.

"There is but one thing that we can do," he said. "We have that disk-like apparatus by which Adams himself went into the interlocking world, and whose purpose I alone here have guessed. With that we can go after him, Harker, can follow him into that interlocking world and, if need be, destroy him, before we allow his terrible work to go on, before our world awakes to find red ruin crashing down upon it. Others would not believe me, would not credit this thing, I know, but you will, Harker. Into that interlocking world went Adams, and after him we two must go!"

I was silent, stunned, at Rawlins' suggestion. The whole thing seemed so fantastic, so incredible, yet I knew that he was right and that it was true; that in that unknown world, locked so strangely with our own, atom within atom, the vengeful Adams was beginning his deadly work, preparing to send God knew what horrors upon the races of man. To venture after him, to burst into that world so near and yet so infinitely far, to cross the vast abyss that separated electron from electron, and plunge into a new, strange world—that was a project appalling in its audacity. But as my brain steadied I saw clearly that Rawlins was right, that we two must follow and find him before he could complete his work of doom, I rose, then, and gave my friend my hand.

"We'll do it," I said, simply. "And God grant that we reach him in time."

THE days that followed live in my memory now as a confused period of swift preparations, many of which were quite incomprehensible to me. Rawlins had examined the great disk-apparatus and had managed to remove it to the little room that was his private laboratory, where we made a further investigation of it. It was long before we could solve the secret of the numberless connections, which joined it to the ray-generators Adams had devised, but when we finally did so, we found that its operation was simple enough. We placed a stone on the lower disk, for a test, and swiftly pulled down the long lever-switch that stood beside it and that governed the intensity of the ray. At once a flood of blinding white light poured down from the upper disk upon the stone, and in an instant it had vanished, while where it had lain was now a little mass of pale blue clay or soil, in which were a few shining, unfamiliar little pebbles, or rocks. It was the corresponding matter of the world locked with our own, transferred into our own as the stone was transferred to that, by the reversal of the motions of its electronic systems, or atoms. As Rawlins pointed out, it was highly important that the ray be turned on at its full intensity, so as to reverse the motion of both electronic systems and transpose them from one world to the other. Were the ray not fully turned on, it would not have power enough to cause that reversal, it would only stop the motion of both electronic systems about their nucleus, resulting in the instant annihilation of both atoms, which is to say, the annihilation of the sections of matter affected in each of the two locked worlds.

We were satisfied with that test, however, and at once set to work to make a duplicate of the transposition apparatus itself, so that we could take this duplicate apparatus with us into the interlocking world and so have a means of returning at will. It was this construction of a duplicate apparatus which proved our hardest task, but we finally achieved it by copying minutely Adams' original apparatus, though much of the work which we did in this way was but little understood by either of us. At last, the duplicate apparatus was complete, and after making a similar test of it, which proved it to be satisfactory, we packed it into as convenient a form as possible and began to hastily assemble the remainder of our equipment.

Rough clothing, heavy automatics, and a supply of concentrated food tablets were the main items in our small outfit, and we took only a few days in assembling it and completing our last preparations. It was near the end of June that we finally found all ready, and prepared to make our start. We had taken nobody into our confidence regarding our plans, knowing well that we should only have been met by the same skeptics and ridicule, which had been allotted to Adams himself. We had given out that we were leaving for a vacation and since we would begin our novel journey in Rawlins' little laboratory, where the big transposition-apparatus was now locked up, we had no fears that our strange departure or absence would be noticed.

At last all our preparations were finished and all was ready for our start. We had agreed to make that start at night. As we walked silently across the campus that evening, toward the great gray stone building that housed our little laboratory, the thing which we were about to do seemed utterly incredible. A June night—with the scent of flowers strong on the soft breeze, with the sound of laughter rippling through the darkness from houses at the campus edge, with the young moon peering down upon us through the trees as we walked on. It seemed fantastic, I thought, that we were actually to venture into a new and unknown world that night. It seemed utterly beyond belief that within minutes more we would be farther from this familiar scene than the farthest of the calm stars above, and yet we would have moved no distance from it at all, at least as we humans think of distance.

Silent with that thought, we walked up into the big building, entered our little room, and after double-locking its door, turned to the apparatus that all but filled the room. The great metal disk on the floor, the similar disk swung ten feet above it, the masses of apparatus grouped beside them—they seemed to be silently awaiting us. It was but the work of a moment to pile our equipment and apparatus neatly upon the lower disk, leaving room for ourselves. Then Rawlins turned toward that disk.

"Time to go," he said, calmly.

With these words he stepped lightly upon the lower disk, and slowly I stepped beside him. We took a last look around the crowded little electric-lit laboratory, and then Rawlins reached toward the big lever-switch that rose on a metal standard beside the lower disk. He grasped it, hesitated a moment, and I felt my breathing tightening, I think that in that moment the same thought, the same icy dread of the unknown, was racing through both our minds. What was awaiting us on the other side, in that strange world locked with ours? The sheer unearthliness of the whole business was gripping us, at the last moment. Suddenly I saw Rawlins' jaw tighten, and he abruptly jerked down the switch.

The next moment there was a blinding glare of light from the disk above us, a light, a force, that flooded down upon us and that in that moment seemed to strike deep into the inmost center of my being, seemed to shake me like a leaf tossed by gigantic winds. Only for a split-second did that light bathe us, and then the little laboratory whirled about me for an instant with immense speed. I seemed to be falling, falling, reeling down through unthinkable abysses, and then light and consciousness alike had left me as I sank into a roaring blackness.

CHAPTER TWO

I OPENED my eyes to a glare of sunlight that caused me to swiftly close them, a white and dazzling illumination that for the moment blinded me, and that beat down upon me with a torrid warmth. In a moment, through half-opened lids, I was able to see that I was lying on the bare ground at the bottom of a small bowl-shaped depression, or crater, with Rawlins lying beside me and our equipment and apparatus lying around us. Then I saw his eyes opening, too, and in a moment more we had got to our feet and were gazing about us.

The first thing that drew my attention was the sun above us. It was of the same size as our own sun, as near as I could judge, but was utterly different. It was blue white and intensely brilliant, its fierce white light and heat a complete contrast to the light of our own yellow star. It was the sight of that strange sun, I think, that first beat into my dazed brain the fact that we had succeeded, and had actually projected ourselves into the world locked with our own. And as Rawlins in turn gazed upward, his face lit up.

"We're there, Harker!" he exclaimed. "We've come through!"

Now, as I gazed about, I saw how unearthly a world it was into which I had come. Standing at the bottom of the little crater, our view was limited by its rim a half-dozen feet above us, but even within its bounds there was difference enough. The ground beneath and around us, we saw, was the same pale blue clay, which we had already seen, and whose tinge had perhaps, some relation to the blue-white sun above us. Here and there in it were white, shining rocks and pebbles, while along the crater's sides were little clumps of vegetation of a deeper blue, strange, twisted little growths, which at first seemed not extraordinary, save for their color. As I watched them, though, I cried out to Rawlins. For the little clumps, I saw, were moving, moving slowly along the crater's side. They had no roots at all, we saw, but had strange little tendrils, which they thrust into the ground as they moved along the barren soil. For all the world they resembled browsing animals, as they slowly passed along, and that, we learned later, was in reality what they were, the barrenness of this world's soil developing in the growths upon it a power to move about and gather their nourishment wherever it might be found.

For the time being, though, we could only guess at that explanation, and watched the browsing plants passing slowly along the crater's side with something akin to horror. In a moment more they had passed up over the crater's rim and had disappeared from view, though still we could catch sight of their blue tips as they moved slowly about, I turned to Rawlins, with the suggestion that we clamber up after them and survey the landscape from the crater's rim, but before the words could pass my lips he had uttered a cry that made me whirl around, and then stand as one transfixed, gazing up with him to the crater's rim above him. For a thing, a creature, had appeared there, whose appearance froze us into a momentary inaction of terror.

I can only describe my first impression of that creature by the statement that it resembled a huge spider, great and black and horrible. There were some eight stiff, jointed limbs, black and smooth and powerful, which combined to support, perhaps five feet above the ground, a black, bulbous mass that was head and body combined, from the bottom of which two additional short and powerful mandibles or arms extended, and from which two strange, dark pupil-less eyes stared down upon us, dark, shining and unwinking eyes whose steady gaze held us there as though hypnotized. Only a moment the thing stood motionless, staring down upon us, and then from an orifice at its bulbous body's base came a high, shrill scraping cry, while at the same moment it hurled itself down the crater's side toward us.

As one in the grip of some terrific nightmare I saw it rushing down upon us, and then it was on us, gripping both of us in an instant with the two short, powerful arms or mandibles, hurling us to the ground. It had gripped me by the throat, and before the paralysis of amazement and fear which had gripped me had vanished, the arm that had grasped me was tightening around my windpipe, squeezing, strangling, choking me, I struck out blindly, helplessly, in that unweakening grip, and heard a hoarse cry from Rawlins as we whirled about on the bottom of the little crater in wild combat with the thing, its dark, unwinking eyes staring dreadfully into our own as we clung and battled together. My senses began to leave me, as that remorseless grip closed tighter around my throat, and then I saw Rawlins' heavy belt-knife flash in his hand, heard another high, shrill cry from the creature that held us and then a dull, ripping sound. The next moment the grip that held me had relaxed, and as I staggered to my feet I saw the thing that had held us slump limply down on to the ground, a black, thick fluid oozing from the side of its bulbous head-body, where Rawlins' knife had pierced it.

He too was scrambling to his feet beside me, and for a moment we contemplated each other, panting and dishevelled, with wild eyes. Then we suddenly stiffened. From above us had come a score or more of high, shrill vibrant cries like that of the creature at our feet, and as we gazed up we saw appear on the edge of the crater, above us, a full two dozen of similar creatures, who stopped there and surveyed us like the first. Some of these, though, carried long, slender, needle-like rods of black metal in their short arms, and these they aimed instantly in our direction. It was plain that they were weapons of some sort, and, as we stood motionless and tense beneath their menace, the spider-creatures came down toward us.

I SAW them inspect the body of the thing at our feet, then one uttered an order, and from one of the needle-like rods there flashed forth a slender bright orange ray, which struck the limp body squarely. As it did so the shattered body vanished at once, beneath our eyes, and the brilliant ray was snapped off. Later we were to learn, what I half-suspected then, that the brilliant orange ray owed its effect to the acceleration of molecular motions which it caused. The molecules, which make up any object are in constant motion, an unceasing motion exhibited by the so-called Brownian movement, and though the object which they make up retains its form without change, it is only because their motions are limited in extent. The orange ray accelerated those motions by causing mutual repulsions between the molecules, which caused them to fly off in every direction, completely annihilating any object that they had made up.

Now, however, we waited tensely, expecting each moment that the brilliant ray would flash forth in destruction toward ourselves, in revenge for the one we had killed, and there was an instant's pause and silence. The whole scene, impressed unforgettably on my brain in that passing moment of stillness, was one of unearthliness beyond all telling. The blue soil, the azure vegetation moving slowly about, the blazing sun whose blue-white brilliance fell upon us, the weird creatures who stood before us—they made up a picture of fantastic grotesqueness, more fantastic, to me, because I knew that even at that instant, at the very spot where we stood, was the familiar, quiet little laboratory which we had left a few moments before, the world of ours so infinitely far from, and yet so closely locked with, this one.

A moment only the things examined us, their strange eyes roving over the equipment and apparatus, which lay about us, and then one stepped forward and swiftly removed from us our weapons and all other objects on our persons. That done, one of them who seemed a leader, uttered a high-pitched, vibrant little cry, pointed with one short arm up toward the crater's rim, and at the same time turned his slender ray-rod full upon us. His meaning was obvious enough, and without answering we started up the little crater's side, preceded and followed by the spider-men, who watched us closely. Looking back, I saw two of them gathering together and bringing with them the equipment and apparatus which lay on the ground.

"There goes our last chance to get back to our own world," I whispered to Rawlins, motioning toward these last two creatures and their burden, but he shook his head.

"We'll get back," he answered, in the same low tones. "And we're in this world, now, where we wanted to be."

I shared none of his confidence, in that moment, but was silent at an imperative gesture from our guards, and continued to climb on upward. This world, I reflected, could not be greatly different in size, at least, from my own, since the force of its gravity was to all appearances the same as that to which I was accustomed in our world. Then I forgot all else as we reached the top of the little crater, where we paused gazing out over the strange vista that lay about us.

It was a barren vista, at first sight, a vast expanse of bare blue soil or earth that swept away to the horizons in great, rolling plains, with neither lake, river nor mountain in sight. Here and there upon it were what were almost its only signs of life, clumps of the same strange vegetation which we had observed in the crater, moving slowly about in search of sustenance from the barren soil, thrusting its multitudinous tendrils into that soil at times and pausing when it found the elements it sought. Except for these, though, the only feature of note in the landscape before us was three strange-looking objects, which lay on the ground perhaps a hundred yards before us.

These seemed at first sight simply square black platforms of smooth metal, lying flat upon the ground, each having a low railing around its edges not more than a foot high. As I gazed at them, though, I saw that at a corner of each there rose a thick, squat cylinder of metal, studded with shining switches. Toward these three platforms, each of which was some ten feet square, our guards motioned us, and as we reached them, we stepped over the low railing upon them, crouching down at their gestures of command. Rawlins and I and some seven or eight of the spider-creatures were upon one of the square platforms, a similar number of the things had taken their place upon another, while the remaining group did not accompany us but stood at a little distance watching us. On our own platform one of the spider-men stationed himself before the thick cylinder in its corner, and began to twist and press the studs upon its surface. A low purring sound rose from the platform's bottom, as he did so, and a moment later the whole flat metal surface rose smoothly into the air.

Straight up it rose, with smooth, effortless speed, until it hovered at a height of a thousand feet above the ground, the other platform rising close beside it. They hovered there a moment, then both swept away toward the north, flashing through the air with rapidly mounting speed, a great wind rising about us and beating upon us as we sped on. Glancing behind I saw the remaining group of spider-men, beside the other black platform on the ground far beneath, apparently watching us depart, and then they had passed from sight behind us and we were racing northward over the great barren blue plains, devoid of any feature of note, save only the occasional patches of moving vegetation and here and there a little bowl-shaped depression or crater like that in which we had been captured.

AS we sped on toward the north, I sought to discover the motive power of the strange vehicle which carried us, and from which came the low hum of power, which was the only sound of operation, I could only conclude that it was developed from forces unknown to us, but later I was to find that the principle of the flying squares was quite simple—it merely made use of the elementary laws of magnetic attraction and repulsion. This world of theirs, like our world, like any world, was a vast magnet, its two magnetic poles attracting unlike poles and repelling like poles. By the apparatus in the cylinder, the spider-men were able to make of the square platform a great magnet, so that it was attracted or repelled by either of the two magnetic poles of their world as they varied the nature of the magnetism with which the cylinder charged it. By skillfully controlling and changing that magnetic charge, they were able to raise the platform; into the air and move it in all directions at will, so that the two platforms were now racing northward, pulled by all the magnetic attractive power of their world's north magnetic pole.

On and on we sped, high above the rolling blue plains, beneath the blazing bluish sun that now was slipping down toward the horizon from the zenith. At last our progress seemed to slacken slightly, and as I raised myself from the crouching position, which we had assumed on the platform's floor, I could make out, far ahead of us, an outline of great black structures, that loomed against the skyline in the distance, which could only be a city of some sort. Toward them our two platforms were flashing on, their speed lessening with each moment, until at last they were within a mile of the city, moving ever more slowly down toward it.

It was indeed a city that I had seen, but a city of a strangeness unparalleled in the universe. I think, a city of cones, black gigantic cones, which rose to a uniform height of a thousand feet or more throughout all the city, mighty cone-shaped structures set on their bases in even rows, ranks, streets, stretching away before us for mile upon staggering mile, into the distance, all of the same size, of the same height, the apex or point of each cut sharply across, truncated, to form a round platform some fifty feet across at the top of each. In scores, in hundreds, in thousands, they sat before us, surrounded by a vast black wall of the same height as they and of tremendous thickness that stretched away on either side from the field of our vision, encompassing all the mighty city. Down toward the city, down toward this huge wall, swept our two flying platforms, and as we dropped closer I saw for the first time the true strangeness and wonder of the place.

For from the flat, truncated top of each of the giant cones, there led out to the tops of the surrounding cone-structures, slender, shining cables of metal, a vast and intricate network of shining threads of communication that led across all the mighty city, connecting cone to cone and cone to wall, as far as the eye could reach. And along those airy cables, along those dizzy ways, there swarmed the hordes of the spider-people, racing from cone to cone on those shining threads without thought of danger, swarming in ceaseless thousands a thousand feet and more above the ground, along those slender cables. These were the streets of this strange city!

While we gazed upon that scene in awe, our two platforms had been dropping down toward the great wall that encircled the city, and in a moment had landed gently upon the flat surface of the mighty rampart, where lay other platforms of the same kind. Now, at a motion of command from our captors, we stepped out, toward the wall's inner edge, where one of the slender, shining cables led from it out toward the nearest of the great cone-buildings. We shrank back as one person from that giddy pathway of the air, but before we could understand their intentions, we had each been grasped by one of the guards, who, holding us tightly in the grip of their two powerful arms, started off from the wall on the narrow cable, out over the city's floor a thousand feet below.

For the moment my heart pounded with fear as they bore us out along that airy way above the city, walking forward on that slender cable as easily as we might have done upon a sidewalk, their multiple limbs grasping it and holding it tightly. I held my breath, still rigid with fear, as they went on, but they seemed not to notice my agitation or that of Rawlins as they went forward. On they went, preceded and followed by our other guards, and in a moment they had reached the flat, round top of the nearest cone-structure, had crossed it, and were moving further in toward the city's center on a similar shining cable. Past cone after cone they went, bearing us tirelessly forward, across the flat tops of the great cone-buildings and along the cables that connected them, meeting and overtaking and passing others of the spider-creatures on those cables, until at last there lay before us a great circular clear space, or plaza, at the city's center, and in the center of which stood a single great cone building of the same size as all the others.

Out from its top there radiated in all directions in-numerable shining cables, connecting it with the buildings of the vast city around it, and now our guards bore us on along one of those cables, toward the central cone-structure's top. As we passed along the cable toward it, I glanced down for the first time, and saw that the spaces on the ground between the great cones were all but deserted, smoothly paved with metal, and that the aerial cables seemed to be almost the sole avenues in use in this strange city. Then we had reached the central building's top, from which scores of the spider-creatures were constantly leaving and on which other scores were as ceaselessly arriving, by the cables. Now, as our guards set us down, we saw before us, at the center of the building's flat, round top, a curious mechanism, whose like I had glimpsed on the building-tops, over which we had already passed, but whose purpose I saw now for the first time.

THE thing was like a great endless belt that rose out of a round black opening near the center of the round flat summit of the great cone, and that moved across that summit for a few feet and then disappeared down into a similar opening at that distance from the first. It was like a broad band of gleaming metal, flexible and endless, that moved smoothly and ceaselessly up out of the one opening, and down into the other, and set along the broad belt's length at every few feet were small curved metal staples, or holds. As we watched, we saw one of the spider-creatures rising out of the opening to our right, clinging to one of the hooks set in it. As the belt bore him upward to the level of the floor on which we stood, he released his hold and stepped out upon that floor, and a moment later was hurrying away from the building on one of the cables behind us. Others of the spider-creatures were ascending and descending by the same method, we saw, making use of this endlessly-moving belt which was apparently the only type of lift or elevator used; by the spider-men in their great buildings. And now our own guards motioned us toward the left-hand opening, into which the endless band descended.

One of them gripped it as it swept past him and a moment later was being carried downward into the darkness of the shaft, motioning with his ray-rod for me to do the same. I hesitated a moment, then grasped one of the holds on the band as it moved smoothly past me, and I too was being swept downward into the darkness, Rawlins and the other guards following me. A moment later the darkness of the shaft gave way to light, as the belt to which I clung shot down into a long, great corridor, into the floor of which the belt vanished through an aperture like that above, while a few feet from it a similar aperture permitted the ascending side of the endless band to rise upward. As he reached the level of the corridor's floor, the guard below me stepped out upon it, and I followed his action. A moment later Rawlins and the other guards were at our side, and we were marched down the long corridor which turned abruptly into a doorway some distance down its length.

We found ourselves in a big room, lit up by high openings in its walls, through which there poured the light of the sinking white sun outside. Shelves and tables littered with scientific apparatus of all sorts filled the room, which had the appearance of a laboratory, while at a desk or bench across the room from us, four figures were standing, intently examining some instrument before them. They turned as we were marched in by our guards, and we saw that three of them were spider-men like our captors, hideous, many-limbed black figures. But it was the fourth figure that held our attention, we stared at him in utter amazement. A human figure! We gasped at the sight of him. It was Adams!

Stunned with surprise, we stood there, gazing at him, while he in turn regarded us with smoldering eyes. To encounter him here, in this strange city of the spider-people, was the last thing we had expected, though it was in search of him that we had come to this strange world. Then, as we gazed, Adams came forward toward us, his burning eyes fixed upon our own.

"So you came after me, Rawlins, into this interlocking world," he said, his voice low but charged with deadly menace. "I thought that perhaps you would—I thought that some might find the apparatus by which I came through to this world, and might dare to follow me, so I gave orders that the spot where I came through be watched. That is why you arrived in the hands of my watchers. You come in time, Rawlins," he went on, his voice suddenly shrill, mad, "I have needed here the help of someone who could understand me perfectly, who could follow my orders in all I have set out to do here, in all that I am doing!"

Rawlins found his voice. "Adams!" he exclaimed. "I came after you because I, at least, know what you are doing, know that already you have made three transpositions of matter from our world to this one, and from this to that."

The mad scientist before him laughed gratingly. "You know that, Rawlins?" he asked. "Then you must know all the rest. Must know that those three transpositions I have already made were but tiny tests. You must know that within days now, when I have completed my work, with your help, it is not mere bits of barren land that I will transpose into that world of yours, that world that derided me. I will transpose cities, the scores of mighty cities of these spider-men, who are weary of this world and to whom I have promised to give the world of man, in exchange for this world, to conquer and destroy and hold it forever. And that is the proof which I shall give to the world that demanded proof!"

He laughed wildly as he finished, and now, as I realized the tremendous horror that loomed above our world, I felt the blood driving from my heart, Rawlins' face had gone dead-white as he listened and now, with a hoarse shout, I saw him leap straight forward toward Adams! I too shouted and sprang to his side, but before I could reach or stay him, the ray-rods of the guards behind us had sprung up and a half-dozen shafts of the brilliant deadly ray were flashing toward us!

CHAPTER THREE

THE moment that followed was to me only a split-second, lightning-like whirl of swift action. At the moment that the deadly orange rays had been released upon us, we had both been leaping forward, and it was that fact alone which saved us, because as we leapt, the brilliant rays grazed past just behind us. Before they could loose the rays again, the spider-men beside Adams had sprung forward and gripped us with their powerful arms, swaying with us there for a moment, and then forcing us back once more, holding us tightly.

Adams came toward us again, his black eyes flaming with the same deadly light. He uttered a series of swift commands in the shrill, vibrant speech of the spider-people, and then spoke to us.

"You will stay here, Rawlins," he said, quietly, "to give me your help when I need it. A little persuasion possibly of a painful sort, will overcome all your scruples, I think. As for Harker, the spider-men can have him. I believe that they have a very interesting method of disposing of their prisoners."

He uttered another shrill, short order, and in answer the guards about us jerked us back to the room's door, back into the long, high corridor. There we were separated, Rawlins being conducted farther down the corridor while two of the spider-guards returned with me along the way we had come. Glancing back, I saw Rawlins' guards halt him farther down the long hall, saw one of them press a stud in it which caused an opening in the wall to appear instantly, a narrow, perpendicular slit that widened swiftly until it was a full-sized door. Through this opening Rawlins was thrust, with a last wave of his hand to me. As the door closed again, I turned back to my own predicament, and found that my two guards had halted me before the ascending side of the endlessly moving belt on which we had descended.

A moment later saw three of us moving smoothly upward on the belt, holding to hooks along its length, and when we had stepped out upon the top of the great cone-building, I saw that darkness was falling upon this giant city of cones, for away to my left, the dazzling white sun was sinking below the horizon. Far below, on the smooth metal paving between the great cones, numbers of the spider-people were moving slowly about, while the traffic on the myriad cables about us seemed to have lessened somewhat. I noticed now, too, what I had failed to observe on my arrival. On the top of this central cone, toward one edge, was gathered a mass of familiar-looking apparatus, very like that which had actuated the transposition machine on which we had come to this interlocking world. Before I could speculate on its presence there, however, one of my guards had grasped me and was moving out upon one of the slender cables that radiated from this central building.

As he moved on I noticed that though the thickening twilight was descending upon the city, great globes of light were shining out, big spheres of shining white light suspended here and there above the tops of the cone-buildings, while other floods of the same white light poured out through the narrow window-openings of those buildings. That illumination was very like the light of the sunken white sun. It was, in fact, as I learned later, sunlight, caught and held during the daytime and released at night. Theoretically, even in my own world, I knew, it would be possible to catch a ray of sunlight between two mirrors, for instance, and keep it reflecting from one to the other indefinitely until it was released. In practice, of course, the imperfections of the mirrors would defeat such a plan. But the spider-men had devised a means by which the vibrations of their sunlight, caught during the day by great light-traps, or lens affairs, were kept stored in a state of unceasing vibration until it was desired to release them as common light once more.

Across all the mighty city, reaching away into the distance on every side, there shone these great white globes of light, but for all their illumination and that which poured from the myriad windows of the great cones, the cables above the city lay in near darkness. Over them, the spider-people still moved unhesitatingly, and now I saw that the guard who was carrying me was reaching the end of the cable, which led from the central cone to one of the circle of cones that lay at the edge of the round plaza in which the central building stood. At last we were upon the top of the building at the cable's end, and as I was set down there by my guard I saw, that, unlike any other of the buildings I had seen in the city, there were upon this building's top a dozen or more of spider-guards, armed with ray-rods, who challenged us in shrill tones as we reached the building's top.

My own two guards answered briefly, and the others stepped aside and allowed us to make our way to the endless belt, which was the one means of ascent and descent in all these buildings. Already I had guessed from the presence of the guards at its top that this building was a prison, and my guess was verified, when after descending halfway down into the building's interior on the great belt, down past a dozen or more levels, we stepped from it upon the floor of another corridor, which, like the others we had come down through on the belt, was patrolled ceaselessly by a half-dozen of the spider-guards. To these again my two captors made brief explanations, then stepped to the smooth wall of the corridor, touched a stud there, and as a narrow, vertical slit appeared in the wall and widened to form a doorway, motioned me through it with their deadly rods.

I stepped inside, slowly and hopelessly enough, and instantly the door began to close behind me, narrowing to a slit and finally disappearing, until only the blank wall was visible. However that strange door was operated, it was as perfect a one for a prison-cell as could well be devised, I turned from it, however, to the interior of my prison, which I found was a small, square room whose only visible opening was a narrow, barred window in the wall opposite me. Through that window there filtered into the dark little room, a feeble white light from the myriad globes of the city outside, and now, by that dim light, I saw that there was another in the room with me, a dark, erect figure, who was coming forward toward me.

For the moment, as it came toward me, I had a wild hope that it was a man like myself who was prisoned here with me, so erect and man-like was that shape as seen in the little room's dim light. But as it came nearer, I shrank back in sudden fear, for this was no man, for all its man-like shape. The erect white body, the two legs or supporting limbs and the two strong upper arms, these were human-seeming enough, but there the resemblance ceased. For though the skin was dull white in color, it was hard and grained in appearance; the arms and the legs both ended in great, three-clawed talons; while the head of the creature, set squarely upon its shoulders, was oddly bird-like, with two small, intelligent dark eyes, a hooked owl-beak between them, which was mouth and nose combined as in any bird, and a thick crest of short white feathers upon the head in place of hair. The only clothing of the creature was a number of leather straps, or belts, about its body. All the fear and awe with which I had first beheld the spider-men returned to me at sight of this strange creature, as it came straight across the cell toward me!

I STOOD silent, hardly breathing, as it came on, thinking for the moment that I had been thrown by the spider-men to the mercy of some strange beast. Then the creature stopped, a sudden curving of muscles wrinkled its face into a grotesque smile, and it spoke to me in deep, guttural tones that were wholly out of place with its bird-like appearance. It was apparently repeating words to me in some unknown language, and as the fear of the thing lessened a little, I smiled in turn. To show that I, too, was an intelligent being, I addressed the creature in my own tongue.

He shook his head, after a moment's thought, pointed to himself, and repeated a few syllables over and over again, still pointing to himself. "Nor-Kan" was what he seemed to be saying, pointing always to himself, and finally I began to understand that he was naming himself, so I in turn pointed to him and repeated the words, at which the grotesque smile re-appeared on his face. Then I followed out the same procedure with myself, pointing to myself and repeating my own name, and within a few moments Nor-Kan, as I had begun to call him, began to understand. Forgetting my own captivity and the enigmatic fate which awaited me, in the interest of this strange creature, I went on in this manner with him through the hours of that night, and by dawn I was still sitting with him in a corner of a little room, learning the words of his strange language by the simple process of having him point to some object, or perform some action, and then repeat for my, benefit the corresponding word or words.

With dawn came one of the spider-creatures, opening the door of our cell a few inches and thrusting in a handful of small brown pellets, which my companion indicated, was food. They were almost tasteless in eating, yet I discovered that they had an extraordinary satisfying power not only for hunger, but thirst as well. Our scanty meal over, I stretched myself on the floor and slept for hours, a sleep broken by nightmares, yet far from the horrible actualities about me. When I awoke, darkness was again settling upon the city outside, and I found my strange companion quietly sitting across the cell and regarding me.

Soon we began our former task of exchanging words and ideas, and within a few hours I had progressed so far in manipulation of the strange gutturals, that we were able to converse in a crude and broken fashion. I pass over the many ludicrous mistakes which I made in the course of our speech, for in spite of these, our progress continued, and by the end of that night I found myself with a rough idea of the situation in this weird interlocking world into which Rawlins and I had come.

Nor-Kan, I found, was of a race totally different from the spider-men, and sharing with them this strange world, the two races being deadly enemies. Ages ago, I learned, the race of Nor-Kan had risen to the position of dominance over this world, as the most intelligent creatures upon it. They had not developed from the mammal races, as did man in our world, but from the bird-races, and though they were still, like Nor-Kan, somewhat bird-like in appearance, they were in reality as far removed from the feathered races from which they had sprung, as man is removed from the great ape-races that were his own progenitors. This race of bird-people had developed a civilization as great as, and greater than, that of man, and over all this world their own cities had stood, while over all other creatures upon it their domination had been established.

Gradually, though, with the increase of their science and their power, the bird-people had softened somewhat, as conquering races will do, and their peoples had less and less desire to perform the various labors of their world. Much of these, it was true, were done by machinery, but much there was that needed directing intelligence, and this was a work for which few of them had any liking whatever. Pressed by the desire of all their peoples, the bird-races' scientists strove to solve the problem set before them, and finally did achieve a solution, which was greatly applauded by the bird-races but which, unknown to them, held within it the seed of their own downfall.

There was among the other creatures of this world a race of spiders, or spider-like creatures, larger than any spiders of earth, but no higher in consciousness and intelligence, and it was in these that the scientists of the bird-races found the solution to their problem. They took individuals of these spider-races and began to alter their very being, changing the nerves and gland-organs in their bodies subtly to make their bodies grow to great sizes, breeding them scientifically one with the other, always with greater intelligence as their goal, and continuing this process onward and onward, until they had developed from these spider-races great spider-creatures, whom they had furnished with powerful arms, and enough intelligence to receive and execute the orders of the bird-people, who could control and direct the machinery of the bird-people without needing their supervision.

Thus were the bird-peoples freed from a great part of their labor, which was now performed by the semi-intelligent spider-men. As time went on, too, these spider-men constantly increased in intelligence under their masters, so that they could take over a greater and greater share of the work of the latter, since it was necessary to increase their mental capacity to ever greater amounts, in order that they could comprehend and execute the increasingly complicated work, which they were now called upon to do. Through the centuries, this process went on, and the result of such a state of affairs might well have been foreseen. There came a day when the spider-servants had attained as much intelligence and science as their masters, whom they greatly outnumbered, and in that day they rose as one and turned upon those masters.

Then there had been flaming revolt and war across all this world, the mighty hordes of the spider-men rising against their masters until but comparatively few of the bird-races were left. These few, some tens of thousands in number, the spider-men had driven steadily back, southward, away from their cities, until only a realm of a few hundred miles about the southern pole remained to the bird-races. There they made their last stand against the spider-men, building their cities there and erecting great barriers around them, which the spider-men, for all their power, could not pass. And in their realm of the southern pole, as habitable beneath the blazing sun as any other portion of the world, the bird-races had stayed, a remnant of their former might, while the spider-men held all the rest of this world, rearing upon it their own strange cities. More than once though, in the centuries that had passed since, Nor-Kan informed me, the spider-men had made attempts to break through the barriers of the bird-races and destroy them, while raiding-parties of the bird-peoples, in turn, still flashed northward occasionally to strike a blow at their ancient enemies. It was on such a raid that he had been captured he told me, having been forced to the ground near one of the spider-cities, as he returned with others from a raid by a defect in the mechanism of his airboat. The airboats of the bird-races, he explained, were wholly different from the flying-platforms of the spider-men being torpedo-like in shape, lifted and flung through the air by a mechanism which cast around them a sheath of invisible vibrations, which were impenetrable to all gravitational force, and by altering which, the craft could be sent at great speed in any direction. He had just repaired the mechanism of his own, he said, when a patrol of the spider-men had pounced upon him and brought him as a prisoner to their city.

"And you've made no effort to escape?" I asked him.

He smiled that grotesque smile. "How?" he asked hopelessly, throwing an arm out toward the solid walls around us, the barred, narrow window. "Even if one could, in some way, open the door of our cell, the corridors outside are constantly patrolled by guards. Even if one got through those corridors and up to the building's top, he would find only more guards there. And if by some miracle one could overcome those guards also, what then? He would still be in the heart of the spider-city, with only those cables leading outward over it, cables and building-tops swarming with the hordes of the spider-men. It is hopeless to try."

I SHOOK my head in stubborn denial, and turned to examine our cell more closely. To escape by its door was obviously impossible, for it was opened only by the stud outside, and presented to us only a blank surface. And as I examined the window, it seemed that it too was hopeless, obstructed as it was by two thick metal bars which were set firmly in the wall at top and bottom. The window itself, as I could see, was, like our cell, halfway up the side of the great cone-building, more than five hundred feet from either the metal paving below or the building's top. To escape through the city below was wholly impossible, I knew. Our only chance was to gain the building's top and somehow make our way to the near-by buildings, where Nor-Kan told me that he had seen his airboat stored. It seemed a madman's scheme to attempt to reach our prison's top, but as I gazed out and saw that at intervals of six feet or more a narrow band or molding encircled the cone-shaped building, I began to see how an escape might be made, wild as the attempt would be.

Swiftly I outlined my scheme to Nor-Kan, and though he shook his head as I unfolded it to him, his eyes were snapping with excitement. When I had finished, he admitted that he might as well perish in making the attempt as wait for the torturing end, which the prisoners of the spider-men inevitably meet within their laboratories. If we gained the top of our prison, we agreed, he was to make an effort to reach and steal his airboat from the nearby cone-top where it was stored, while I was to venture back toward the central building where Rawlins had been imprisoned and attempt to free him, awaiting Nor-Kan on that building's top. The whole scheme seemed as mad a one as could possibly be devised, but it was at the same time our one chance for life and liberty. We began to work upon it at once, turning our attention toward the window-bars, which obstructed that opening.

To sever those bars was the thing upon which all our scheme rested. Luckily we had a crude means of doing so. Though Nor-Kan had been stripped of all his possessions, just as I had been, his captors had overlooked the heavy metal buckles of the leather harness, being attracted by the weapons which he wore. These buckles were long, with finely serrated edges of hard metal, crude little miniature saws, in fact, made so as to make more secure the weapons and tools, which were sometime hung upon them. In a moment we had disengaged two of the buckles, and with their edges had set to work upon the bars, at their bases. Dawn was breaking again upon the city outside, and we ceased our work until the door had opened and our strange food had been thrust in. Then we turned again to the bars and sawed furiously at the thick metal.

Through all of that day we worked on at the two thick bars, stopping only now and then for a moment of rest, and when darkness came again had almost severed them. A few more hours of work followed, which we could carry on only by the faint light that fell upon us from the great radiant white globes scattered here and there across the city, and then at last we had cut through both the bars. That done it was but the work of a few minutes; exerting all our strength on each bar in turn, to bend them inward and to one side. Then I leaped upon the sill of the narrow opening, and sat for a moment straddling it, gazing cautiously out over the scene before me.

Before me lay the great panorama of the city of the spider-men, a forest of dark, gigantic cones whose openings gleamed with white light. To my right lay the circular clearing at the city's center where stood the single cone that was the prison of Rawlins, and looking up I saw that only a few spider-creatures, here and there, were moving over the many cables. Beneath me the slanting wall of the great cone dropped downward at a sharp angle toward the metal paving below, upon which there moved a few of the spider-men, though for the most part they seemed to retire within their great buildings at the coming of night. I glanced downward, then upward where the great wall slanted sharply up above me, and then gently swung myself out of the narrow window until my feet were resting precariously upon the narrow band or molding just below the window, one of the similar bands, either ornamental or to increase the structure's strength, which encircled it at intervals of six feet or more from its base to its truncated tip.

The molding was not more than an inch in thickness, and for an agonizing moment while I teetered upon it, I was reaching upward toward the next band above it. As my hands finally gripped that band, Nor-Kan was emerging from the window beside me, and a moment later I felt his powerful arms pushing me slowly up the steeply slanting side of the great building, up until my feet were resting upon the narrow band which my hands had clutched a moment before. Then, grasping one of the straps about his body, I slowly pulled him up beside me, and in another moment we clung together to the narrow foothold. And then I was reaching upward again toward the encircling band above us.

THE time that followed, while we crawled in this way up the side of the mighty building like two strange insects, was, I think, the most agonizing in all my life. Upward we went, from band to band, clinging with all our strength to our inch-wide foot and hand-holes, pushing and pulling each other in turn up the side of the gigantic cone, avoiding all the openings in its side as we clambered slowly upward. We were within a hundred feet of the great cone's top, and hopes of success were beginning to rise within me, when suddenly, as I stooped slightly to pull Nor-Kan up to the narrow band on which I was standing, my feet seemed to slip beneath me upon that band, and instantly I was reeling downward!

Had the building's sides been vertical, nothing could have saved me from a hideous death on the metal paving hundreds of feet below, but the steep slope of the great cone's sides saved me. For before I had fallen a half-dozen feet I was scraping along the steeply slanting side in my fall, and as I did so my hands caught, automatically and entirely without conscious thought, upon one of the narrow bands up which we had come. The narrow band was no more than enough to give a hold to my fingertips and for a moment I clung there with all the energy of despair. I felt my hold giving, as I swung gently to and fro, felt my cramped fingers straightening, slipping, and then as they gave up their holds nervelessly, my hands were gripped by strong talons from above, and within another moment Nor-Kan had pulled me up beside him.

For minutes we clung there without moving, lying inward against the slant of the great building, while I regained my breath, and overcame the violent trembling that had seized me, and then we took up our climb again. Still up and up we went, from band to band until at last we were within a few yards of the cone's flat, round top. There came down to us through the darkness from that top, the sound of shrill, high voices and the occasional sound of shuffling limbs, so that we knew the guards were there and watchful. Slowly; stealthily, we made our way upward, and finally had reached the last of the encircling bands. Standing upon it, we could raise our eyes cautiously above the level of the building's top.

Upon it, we saw now, were about a dozen of the spider-men, all armed with the deadly ray-rods, conversing desultorily amongst themselves, while one or two moved restlessly about. The white globes of light suspended here and there above the city, shed a clear light upon the scene, and we saw that it was madness to show ourselves upon the great cone's top. Just above us, though, within our reach, there stretched the shining, slender cables that led from the cone's top out, to the near-by buildings, and it was to reach these that we had risked our lives in our great climb up the building's side. Silently, still clinging to the upmost band, we began to move around the building.

On we went, with slow, stealthy progress, but before we had gone a dozen feet one of the buckles of Nor-Kan's straps flapped inward and clanked with a metallic sound against the building's wall. At once we flattened ourselves against that wall, praying that the sound was not heard, but even as we did so, there came the sound of shuffling feet or limbs as one of the spider-guards above crossed the round platform toward the edge where we crouched. Were we discovered, a single push would send us both down to a fearful death a thousand feet below, we knew, and we held our breath as the shuffling steps came closer.

The creature could hardly have been more than a few feet from the edge just above us when from one of the other spider-men on the building's top came a shrill call. The guard who had been moving toward us to investigate paused, and after a tense moment, retraced his steps towards the others of the group, where we heard him joining in their conversation. We drew long breaths, and then started on, around the edge of the great building's top toward the cables we sought.

In a moment more I had reached the cable which led out toward the top of the cone in the central clearing, and as I paused there, Nor-Kan crept on and then he too paused beside another of the cables, indicating to me that it was the one he had sought. Then, gripping it with his strong taloned hands, he started to swing himself along its length through the darkness. In a moment more he had disappeared into that darkness, and summoning all my resolution, I grasped the slender cable just above me with my own hands, and with a silent motion swung myself from my precarious position on the building's side out into empty space, hanging from the cable with more than a thousand feet of empty air between myself and the hard metal surface far below.

Hand over hand, outward I swung along the slender cable, out into the darkness toward the top of the central cone, hundreds of yards away. At any moment I expected a shrill cry from the guards on the roof behind me to herald my discovery, but the shrouding darkness hid me from their eyes, and as I swung on, I felt a rising hope that I might yet succeed. Far below I could glimpse the metal paving, glinting dully in the light of the white globes of light throughout the great city. I could glimpse upon it a few of the spider-creatures moving from building to building, while here and there on the myriad cables about me I half caught sight of other dark spider-shapes moving along those shining threads.

On and on I swung, until I had crossed half the gulf that lay between the two great buildings, but by then I felt such overpowering fatigue in my arm muscles that, for a few moments, I swung from the cable by my knees to give my arms a slight rest. Then, reaching up again, I swung on my way once more, hand after hand, but before I had gone a dozen feet farther I stopped abruptly and hung motionless. From ahead of me, along the cable, came a slight scurrying sound that chilled my blood. For as I hung there I saw the figure of a spider-man coming toward me, out of the darkness. On he came along the cable, suddenly saw me hanging there, a thousand feet in mid-air, and as he did so, he stopped short, and gazed at me. Then he uttered a shrill cry, seemed to gather himself, and was leaping forward along the cable, straight toward me!

CHAPTER FOUR

I THINK now that the paralysis of fear that gripped me could have lasted for only the briefest possible moment, but at the time it seemed eternities to me as I watched that dark, hideous shape flashing along the cable toward me as I hung helplessly. Before it could reach me, though, enough of my presence of mind had returned to me and I swiftly swung up, and buckled my knees again about the cable, just as the creature grasped me by the body, clinging to the cable with its own multiple limbs, while I in turn strove for a hold on the hideous bulbous mass that was both its head and body.

In a moment I had grasped it, and then, locked in a death-grip, we swung there on the slender cable, struggling silently in the shrouding darkness, far above the ground. In utter, deadly stillness we swung and twisted there, while all about and below us the white-lit openings of the great cones and the radiant globes above them gleamed through the darkness like great white eyes staring at us. Exhausted as I was, though, I knew I was no match in strength for the creature with whom I struggled, and at last I felt myself being slowly lifted up by his powerful arms, away from my desperate hold upon the cable.

Up I was lifted, up and sidewise, until I felt the last of my grasp on the cable going, and knew that a moment more would see me hurled down to death below. Nothing could save me, I knew, and at the thought such a mad despair and fury surged through me, that, filled with a wild resolve to take my opponent with me to death, at least, I suddenly released my last hold on the cable and threw myself bodily upon him.

It was the last thing that he had expected me to do, this sudden mad attack on my part, and it took him so by surprise, that before he could make certain of his own grip on the slender cable, my leaping rush had knocked him sidewise from it. He tottered, swayed, and then with a thin scream fell abruptly and whirled downward into the darkness. For the moment I thought that I too was tottering to my doom, but as I had thrown myself upon my enemy, my elbows had caught on the cable, sustaining me for an instant while he fell, and in the next moment I had reached up and was again hanging from it with my knees, shuddering violently. Hanging there, head downward, I could make out on the metal street far below a black little blotch that I knew was the body of my opponent, but as the ways below were all but deserted, it was my hope that it would not be discovered for minutes, at least.

I knew, though, that my time was short, and in a moment reached up again, and swung on along the cable's length toward the central cone, hand over hand, along that airy pathway, until within a few more minutes I had reached the top of the central cone and was scrambling upon it, breathing a sigh of relief to find it for the moment deserted. On one side of it, was the mass of apparatus I had noticed before, around which a low metal railing had been constructed, and my heart leaped as I saw that the apparatus was in reality a partially-constructed duplicate of the one which had propelled us into this strange interlocking world. The coils and generators and switches were of the same sort, I noticed, but all were far larger in size, and instead of the two big metal disks of our machine, there was, what appeared to be a metal globe, or world-map, different points of which, movable pointers attached to the intricate masses of apparatus were touching. The whole affair seemed incomplete, as yet, and before its full significance could strike me, I had leaped on toward the endlessly ascending and descending belt, and in another moment was being carried downward by that belt into the interior of the mighty building.

Down it swept me, into the darkness, and then into light, the same long and shadowy corridor where my guards had halted me on my former visit there. As I reached the floor of that corridor, which seemed quite silent and deserted, I sprang quietly off the belt, and then crept forward toward the open door of the laboratory in which Adams had confronted us, and from which a stronger white light was pouring out into the more dimly lit hall, I could hear voices from the inside of that laboratory, high, shrill and vibrant voices, and cautiously I crept to its doorway and peered inside.

In it were Adams and two of the spider-men, busy now about a smaller piece of apparatus similar to those I had seen on the building's top. As they worked upon it they conversed in their odd, high tones. Quietly, I waited there, until they had turned for a moment from the direction of the door, and then slipped silently past it, and hurried on down the long corridor, pausing before the section of the wall through which I had seen Rawlins thrust. After a moment's feeling in the shadows, I found the stud on the wall and pressed it. Instantly a narrow slit appeared in the wall, widening into a doorway, and as I stepped into the little room beyond it, there was a rustle as its occupant rose to meet me. It was Rawlins, his face wondering in the dim light, and when he saw my own, he uttered a low exclamation that I silenced with an upraised warning hand.

"Harker!" he whispered. "How did you get here—"

"Quiet, Rawlins," I told him. "We've got a chance to get free if we can get to the building's top." And briefly I whispered to him of the plan of Nor-Kan to meet us there with his airboat if he could manage to steal it.

He nodded quickly, his eyes afire, and then motioned me ahead. Once out of the room we set off down the corridor, as silently as possible. In a moment we had reached the edge of the laboratory door, from inside of which there came the shrill voices of Adams and the spider-men, I turned, was about to motion to Rawlins to make a leap with me across the door, when the voices inside came abruptly nearer, and within another instant the three were emerging from the laboratory into the corridor!

BEFORE we could think of retreating down the hall, they were outside, and we had time only to throw ourselves backward to the floor into the shadows, and crouch there in silent prayer that we might not be seen. As we did so, the three had come out of the door, the two spider-men starting off down the corridor in an opposite direction to ours, while Adams, after calling something after them in his harsh, shrill tones, moved back into the white-lit laboratory. In a moment more the two spider-men had disappeared from view around a bend in the corridor, and we breathed heartfelt sighs of relief. I motioned to Rawlins to proceed toward the belt-stairway now, but he held me back, his face suddenly alight with excitement.

"Adams is alone, in there," he whispered tensely. "It's a chance in a thousand for us to get him, take him as a prisoner with us!"

My heart quickened uncontrollably at the suggestion, but I saw the force of it. With Adams our prisoner, we could halt the completion of his deadly work, could prevent the catastrophe that loomed for our world. "We'll try it," I whispered, "but if he sees us and cries out before we get him, it's all up with us."

Now we crept to the doorway, gazed inside, Adams had returned to the long desk and was again examining the apparatus upon it on which he had been working. His back was turned toward us, and silently we crept into the room, moving forward inch by inch, drawing nearer him like wild beasts stalking their kill. Inch by inch we moved on, silently, stealthily, until at last we were within a few feet of him, were moving forward upon him with upraised hands. And then, warned by some strange instinct, he suddenly turned full toward us!

His eyes widened as he saw us, and then, even in the instant that we gathered ourselves for a spring upon him, he had given utterance to a high, shrill cry, a vibrant call that echoed through the great building's corridors and halls and was taken up and repeated by scores of other voices. Even at the moment that he cried out Adams had whirled to one side with astounding quickness, was springing out of the door and down the long corridor, and as we leaped after him, Rawlins turned to me, his face livid.

"No chance now!" he cried. "The building's top's our last chance!"

Toward the great ascending and descending belt we ran, while farther down the corridor we saw Adams racing on, a babble of shrill cries loosed throughout the building now in answer to his calls. We reached the ascending side of the belt, grasped the hooks in it, and as we were carried smoothly upward, we saw Adams turning, and with a crowd of the spider-men aroused by his cries, he came running down the corridor toward us. Then they passed from our sight as we were carried on up into the darkness and then into the light again as we came out upon the flat, round top of the great cone-building. It was quite clearly lighted by one of the near-by radiant white globes, and I saw at once that there was no sight of Nor-Kan or his airboat upon it. He had failed, and our last chance was gone with him!

The despair and bitterness of approaching death settled upon me, as I felt that our fate was sealed, but now I heard a cry from Rawlins, saw him leap to the little metal railing that surrounded the apparatus beside us, saw him tear a section of that railing away by main force, a long metal bar, with which he leapt toward the ascending belt up which we had just come. Even as he did so, one of the spider-creatures, a ray-rod in his grasp, aimed toward us, appeared on that belt. Before he could release its deadly force, Rawlins' heavy metal bar had crashed down upon him and sent him reeling back down into the shaft in a crushed, limp mass.

I tore a bar from the railing for myself and leaping to Rawlins' side, saw a half-dozen of the spider-creatures ascending in a close group, clinging to the endlessly moving belt. Their brilliant orange rays shot up toward us as they were carried upward but we had stepped back and they could not reach us with the ray from the interior of the shaft. The next moment they had been carried up to its mouth, and then, before they could again release the rays, our two bars had smashed down as one and they too were tumbling downward in a shattered mass of dead and dying. Still they continued to whirl up toward us on the great belt, singly, in groups, in masses.

The moments that followed were moments of madness. Up and downward our great clubs were whirling, smashing through the bulbous bodies as though through eggshells, sending them down into the shaft in masses of shattered dead, while all about us, it seemed, there hissed and flashed the brilliant orange molecular rays with which the spider-men strove in vain to reach us from the shaft. We heard Adams' voice, urging them on from beneath, but they needed no urging for the belt carried them endlessly up toward us. Such a battle could not last for long, I knew, even while I whirled and struck, for now the city was aroused all around us; shrill cries and alarms were spreading across it, new white lights were flashing into sudden being.

By those lights I could glimpse, all across the city, it seemed, scores of the spider-creatures leaping toward us along the shining cables, racing across those airy ways above the city toward the top of our central cone. A moment more and they would be upon us, a moment more and their deadly rays would stab forth to annihilate us, I knew. But even at that moment there came a hoarse cry from beside me, and I saw that one of the spider-men on the ascending belt had managed to snatch the end of Rawlins' bar as he struck, had torn it from his grasp and struck him back a blow that sent him to his knees at my side. Before the spider-man could strike again, my own bar crashed down upon him, and I stooped to my friend's side, half-raised him to his feet. Now, amid a wild babble of fierce, shrill cries, the hordes from below were sweeping up toward us on the belt unopposed, Adams at their head, while the other hordes upon the cables were racing along the last few yards of their length toward our building top. From beneath, from all about us, the dark spider-hordes rushed upon us, as I half-raised Rawlins to his feet. It was the end, I knew.

Then suddenly a dark, long shape seemed to swoop down out of the upper darkness into the white light at the great cone's top, a strange, long shape, upon which I glimpsed a dark figure, a grotesque and bird-like figure at sight of which I shouted aloud.

"Nor-Kan!" I screamed, and even as I did so, I saw his long airboat drive down beside us, felt his strong grasp pulling us up beside him. Then, as a score of brilliant rays leapt toward us from the spider-men on the cables and those pouring up on the great belt, the airboat soared sharply up with immense speed, clear of the deadly rays, and in a moment the wild melee on the building-top beneath had dwindled and died in our ears as we flashed upward and outward into the night.

Now, as the long, torpedo-shaped little airboat soared over the great cone-city of the spider-men, its white globes of light beaconing the darkness beneath us, I turned to Rawlins, and found that save for a slight stunning, he had been unhurt by the blow that had felled him. I turned to Nor-Kan, who was at the controls beside me, and returned the smile with which he greeted me.

"You came just in time," I told him. "I thought it was all up with us—that you'd failed to get to your airboat."

"It was a close thing," he said, "but I managed to get to it." And then he told us, (I interpreted for Rawlins) how he had swung along the cables after leaving me, toward the cone-top where his airboat lay, making his way to it as I had done, but without my misadventure and combat in mid-air. He had been forced to hang from the edge of the building for many minutes, he told me, before a chance turning away of the spider-guards on its top had given him a chance to spring up and leap into his airboat, slanting up into the darkness before the surprised guards could prevent him, and swooping down upon the cone-top where we battled, just in time to save us.

WHILE we talked, the little airboat had been driving toward the south at immense speed, and minutes before the last lights of the great city of cones had vanished in the darkness behind us. Now a pale light was welling up from the horizon at our right, the white light of dawn. As it intensified swiftly we saw that our airboat was driving southward high above the rolling blue plains, with none of the spider-men or their cities now in sight. As the light increased, though, Nor-Kan turned for a moment from the little craft's controls, gazing anxiously backward.

"You think they're following?" I asked, and he nodded slowly.

"None of their flying-platforms are swifter than this airboat," he said, "but the city from which we escaped will flash word to all their southernmost cities, on a light-beam system of communication which they have, to watch for us and cut us off as we make for the south. Our only chance is to get to the south-polar realm of my people and inside its barrier before the flying platforms can find us."

With these words he turned back to the airboat's controls, and we kept a tense and constant watch upon the surrounding horizons as hour after hour the little craft flew south. Nor-Kan, as he told us, was increasing the distance of our flight by taking a zigzagging course to avoid the cities of the spider-men, which lay about us, so that, while we drove southward, the blue-white sun mounted to the zenith, and then was declining again. Far beneath us the surface of this weird world slipped by, the great blue barren plains, the occasional depressions or hillocks that varied their appearance, the great masses of azure vegetation which moved slowly and restlessly about beneath us, browsing here and there. Some of the time I spent in imparting to Rawlins the rudiments of the strange language of the bird-peoples which I had learned, but for the most part we occupied ourselves in scanning the air about us for the enemies who we knew were near. Twice, we glimpsed far in the distance, moving black specks that we knew were scouting flying-platforms seeking us but each time Nor-Kan sent the airboat down toward the ground to hover motionless until our enemies had passed from sight. A cordon of these scouting platforms would have been drawn up to prevent our escape to the south-polar realm of the bird-races, we knew, and we knew also that to slip through that cordon would be a difficult task.

At last, though, late in the afternoon, Nor-Kan turned to us with some relief on his face. "I think that we've got through them all," he said. "We're south of the last spider-city, now, and within an hour we'll be at the barrier of my own land. Within an—"

He stopped abruptly, the words dying on his lips, as he gazed past us to the right and behind us. We turned, alarmed, and for the moment we stood as appalled as he. Away to one side and behind, speeding after and toward our airboat in an oblique course, were a half-dozen square black shapes that were now no more than a half-mile from us.

"Scouts of the spider-men!" cried Nor-Kan. "If they overtake us before we get to the barrier we're lost!"

He whirled to the craft's controls, opened its speed lever to the last notch, and sent the airboat racing on toward the south in a burst of added speed. The great flying-platforms swiftly leapt after us, hurtling through the air at immense speed and slowly drawing ever closer toward us moving obliquely toward our own course. Closer they came, and closer, airboat and flying-platforms cleaving the air at a velocity unthinkable; now we saw from the foremost of the platforms behind us a shaft of brilliant orange light that burned toward us as at the same moment Nor-Kan swerved the airboat to avoid it. He turned toward us, motioned swiftly toward the long, tube-like projector mounted on a swivel at the stern of our own airboat, and which I had already noticed.

"The static-gun!" he cried. "There are a few charges left in it—try to stop them with it!"

I sprang to the weapon and hastily, at the shouted direction of the bird-man, aimed the long tube at the foremost of our pursuers, and then pressed the button at its base. Instantly a little shining metal cartridge flicked out of the long tube and whizzed through the air to strike the foremost of the flying-platforms squarely. As it did so it seemed to burst, to expand into a faint glow of light that enveloped the flying-platform from end to end. The next moment, from the ground far below, a terrific and blinding flash of lightning had sprung upward and struck the faintly glowing platform, sending it reeling down in a flaming, shattered mass by that tremendous discharge. The principle of the weapon, as I guessed, was that of the lightning itself, since the missiles it fired contained great charges of static electricity which enveloped whatever object they broke against, giving to that object a powerful electric charge which caused an instant electrical discharge or lightning-bolt, from the ground up toward it, just as a lightning-bolt or so-called "backstroke" will sometimes burst up from the charged earth toward a charged cloud, just as a lightning-bolt or electrical discharge will flash from one charged cloud to another, or from a cloud to earth.

AS the foremost of them was destroyed thus, our pursuers seemed to waver a moment to slacken their speed a little, and then they leaped forward again toward us, their brilliant rays reaching and questing through the air in search of us, while Nor-Kan drove the airboat up and about in swift, erratic evolutions to escape those rays. I saw him pointing ahead, as he did so, saw far ahead a mass of slender, soaring white towers that glistened brilliantly in the sunlight, and that stretched far away on either hand, I knew that we were approaching the polar land of the bird-peoples, and as we flashed on in mad flight from our relentless pursuers, I could understand the nature of the mighty barrier, which the bird-races had erected all about their land to bar the hordes of the spider-men forever.

It was a barrier invisible, almost. It could be seen only by a slight flicker in the air that the eyes could hardly catch, but it manifested itself to our ears in a tremendous roaring sound that grew in titanic volume as we sped on toward it. For it was a barrier of winds that encircled the realm of the bird-people, a wall of tremendous, ceaseless winds that roared upward from the ground unceasingly with incalculable speed and power, caused by the bird-people by encircling their land with a sheath of the same gravity—opaque vibrations which propelled their airboats, and which, projected on the ground in a great circle about their land caused the air above that circle to rush violently upward, freed of its own weight and pressed by the weight of the air on either side, rushing up in a mighty wall of inconceivably powerful blasts which nothing could hope to penetrate, up toward the limits of the atmosphere itself. And we were rushing madly on toward this barrier now, with the remaining flying-platforms close on our track.

Their rays were still slicing the air about us as we sped on, and it was only by a miracle that we escaped them in that moment. I again swung the static-gun toward the platforms, sent another of the deadly missiles whizzing back toward them, and another, and another, before the exhausting of its few charges made the gun useless. The first two of my shots went wild as the platforms behind dipped suddenly, but the third caught one of them as it rose again, and it too, glowed faintly with the sudden charge from the missile, another shattering blast of lightning ripped up from the ground far below to annihilate the platform and all upon it. Even as it whirled downward, though, the deadly orange ray from one of its fellows had swung across our own ship, and though Nor-Kan swerved sidewise with the speed of light, almost, the brilliant ray sliced down across our airboat's side, annihilating a section of that side, so that our speed slowed considerably. Ahead now the mighty walls of winds, roaring upward like the unceasing thunder of doom, and drowning every other sound, was not a thousand yards away, and from the ring of little white projector-stations which controlled it, inside of it, we could see bird-men running out, gazing toward us in excitement. But behind us, now, the platforms of the spider-men were leaping ever closer toward us, their rays no longer in action as they crowded to their platforms' sides, to board and capture us.

Closer they sped on our track, and now were but a scant hundred feet behind us, leaping closer and closer. Nor-Kan, his face set, was driving straight toward the mighty barrier of winds, in which our craft could not live an instant, I knew. Beside us we saw Rawlins' mouth, evidently voicing a cry which I could not hear for the thunderous roaring of those winds. We had almost reached them, now, sucked forward by the onrushing currents that fed them from either side, the platforms behind still whirling after us, and then I half-closed my eyes as our airboat plunged in toward its death in those terrific currents.

But as it did so the mighty roaring abruptly ceased, the winds for the moment vanished, as the gravity-sheathing vibrations which caused them were suddenly switched off, inside. We rocketed through and over the projector stations inside, and then the next moment the vast currents were thundering upward again with all their former power, while the pursuing platforms of the spider-men, a hundred feet behind us, drove straight into that terrific barrier.

We saw them whirl sidewise with lightning-like speed as though jerked up by a giant hand, saw them crumpling and collapsing as the vast winds whirled them upward, and then they had vanished far above, smashed utterly and flung upward in less than a second of time, by that mighty wall of moving air through which nothing, Nor-Kan had truly said, could ever pass and live.

Now, as our own airboat drove in over the ring of projector-stations from which the barrier had been switched off so opportunely for us, I saw that from the city of white towers ahead swarms of other airboats like ours, many of them much larger, had risen and were speeding toward us. Rapidly Nor-Kan hailed them, and as they turned to carry back to the city news of our arrival, we limped on toward that city in our battered craft.

A far-flung mass of soaring white towers it gleamed, in the light of the descending sun, and in the distance beyond it I glimpsed other masses of similar towers, other cities of the bird-people, all gathered here behind the impenetrable barrier in this polar realm that was their last refuge. Now, as our craft slanted down into the city, down between the soaring towers toward the base of the greatest of them, I saw that in the wide streets beneath us were gathered masses of the bird-people, all of the same appearance as Nor-Kan.

As our airboat came to rest at the base of the mighty building, we stepped off it, into those swarming, wandering masses, as grotesque-seeming to our eyes as we must have been to theirs, and were led by bird-men whose leather straps bore a peculiar insignia, into the building before us. There, with Nor-Kan, we were conducted into a long, bare white room, with high ceiling and high-arched windows, in which the only furniture was a great rectangular white block at the room's center, about which, as about a table, were grouped a dozen or more square seats.

At the end of the block was seated a bird-man of the same appearance as all the others we had seen, but with a commanding aspect and expression which silently proclaimed him a person of authority. He greeted Nor-Kan calmly as he entered, spoke to us with an interest and wonder his features could not conceal, and then turned from us as into the room a dozen or more other bird-men entered, whom he also greeted briefly, and who then seated themselves, with us, around the great block-table at the room's center.

NOR-KAN had informed me that this was the ruling committee of the races of the bird-men, each of their cities being represented upon it, and that it was in response to his own summons that the members had been hastily assembled. Now, as they seemed to wait in silence, he rose to address them. He told them briefly, of his own capture by the spider-men, of his meeting with me, and of our hazardous escape from the spider-city. He stressed the fact that Rawlins and I had come from a world interlocking with their own, and though there was wonder on the faces of the birdmen, I saw that their own science was great enough to enable them to appreciate the possibility of the two worlds interlocking in this manner. Then Nor-Kan explained that Adams, a human like ourselves, had joined the spider-men, and was planning to transpose all their cities, all the hordes in those cities, into our own world to conquer and destroy, having set up ray-projectors for that purpose beneath each of the spider-cities, and being now engaged in completing the central control for all those projectors, which was located on the top of the central cone where we had confronted Adams. That central cone itself, as Nor-Kan told them, would not be transposed into the interlocking world, being, protected from the rays, but all the city around it and all the other cities of the spider-men would be so transposed.

"And that means defeat and destruction for ourselves as well as for Rawlins and Harker and their races," said Nor-Kan. "Hitherto our mighty barrier of winds has kept the spider-men from entering our realm, since none of their flying-platforms could ever pass it, and our cities and stations from which it is projected are set too far back from it for their molecular rays to reach. But if they burst into this interlocking world of Rawlins and Harker, then all that they will need to do is to fly south to the polar regions of that world and be transposed back into this one, and they will be inside our barrier, leaping upon us and destroying us. There is but one chance for the races of the bird-peoples, and that is to destroy the ray-projectors which Adams has built to transpose their cities into the interlocking world, and to do that we must gather all our forces and sail north, must swoop down on the city where Adams is working now at the completion of the controls of his deadly mechanisms, and must destroy them before he can finish them, before they can flash the spider-cities and all their hordes into the interlocking world."

There was a silence in the room when Nor-Kan's deep voice had ceased, a strange stillness broken only by the hum of distant voices that came whispering into the room from the anxious masses of the bird-people that had gathered in the streets outside. In the decision of the committee and its leader, we knew, there rested the fate of both interlocking worlds and in a tense silence Rawlins and I waited for that decision. At last the bird-man at the table's end rose and slowly spoke.

"For age upon age," he said, his deep voice vibrating through the room, "we races of bird-peoples have clung to our refuge here at the southern pole, have sheltered ourselves behind our barrier while our ancient enemies, the servants whom our own ancestors developed to be their doom, have mastered all the rest of this world, which once we mastered. Fewer than the spider-men in numbers, pressed by their hordes down into this last refuge at the southern pole, we have not thought of attacking them in force, but have been content to defend ourselves. But now, as Nor-Kan has told you, we must attack and defeat them, or perish. So that now, as ruler and leader of the races of bird-peoples, I say that all our forces shall be gathered together here as swiftly as they may be gathered, and shall sail north to attack the spider-men and destroy the deadly thing that Adams has built for them, shall flash north to strike with all our power the one great blow which alone can save from the spider-men the two interlocked worlds!"

CHAPTER FIVE

As our craft slanted up into the sunlight above the towering city of the bird-peoples, two days after our arrival at that city, I saw, rising below and beside us, score upon score of long airboats like our own, literally hundreds of craft, each manned by a score or more of bird-men. During the two days we had spent in their city those fleets of ships had been gathering there, racing on in answer to the call from each of the bird-people's cities in this strange realm at the pole. More than a thousand in number, they had massed at this northernmost city of the bird-people, each ship equipped with static-guns and with other weapons that had been hastily devised for them.

During those two days, too, Rawlins and I had seen but little of the city of the bird-people, for Nor-Kan had been appointed as leader of the whole fleet, and we were busy with him in devising a plan of attack. We had decided that our best plan would be to head straight toward the spider-city, where we had been imprisoned, and where we knew Adams was laboring to complete the controls of his apparatus on the central cone, to transpose to our earth the spider-cities and their hordes. Once at that city we were to sacrifice all else to destroy that central cone and the deadly apparatus upon its top, and it was our hope that by the fury of our attack this end might be accomplished.

Now, as Rawlins and I stood with Nor-Kan on the sunken, sheltered deck of the long airboat that was the flagship of the fleet, we could see all our myriad of craft rising around us, slanting up with us until the great fleet hovered momentarily above the soaring white towers of the city of the bird-people. Swiftly, as the signals flashed from our own craft, the airboats gathered themselves into a fighting formation, arranging themselves in three long lines not far apart, and then, as another signal flashed, the whole fleet, with our flagship in the front, began to move out over the city, smoothly and silently, toward the north.

Looking down I saw the streets and squares of the splendid city below us thronged with crowded masses of its inhabitants, watching in silence as their silent fleet moved out to battle. Glistening, shining, in the brilliant morning sunlight of the blue-white sun to our left, the hundreds of long, graceful craft were an inspiring sight as they moved steadily forward, and I saw pride in the eyes of Nor-Kan as he glanced back over the shining files that followed us.

"Never before has such a force of my race gone out against the spider-men," he said to us, "and for that reason our attack, I think, will be a complete surprise to them, so that we can swoop down upon them before they're aware of our presence."

I nodded, without answering, for by this time we were approaching the great wall of winds whose thunderous roar made all speech difficult. Nearer we sailed toward it, high above the ground, and the roaring of the mighty, invisible barrier was deafening, when abruptly as before, it ceased, the winds subsiding, as the projected vibrations opaque to gravity, which caused them, were snapped off to allow us to pass. Onward our fleet smoothly sailed; through the air where the wall had been, and then, as the last of our ships came through and beyond its circle, the vast winds again sprang into sudden being, roaring upward again with renewed and deafening power.

Now our fleet was moving faster, was rising into the air, until we were flashing northward almost at full speed, and at a height of perhaps a mile above the ground. Behind us the towers of the bird-men's polar cities faded out of sight, while we sped north above the blue plains toward the spider-city that was our goal. Far below we could make out the same weird landscape over which we had flashed on our wild flight southward, the strange vegetation that moved on it, being the only sign of life, as before. Hour after hour, we sped on, evading the southernmost cities of the spider-men as we had done on our own escape, heading straight toward the city where was Adams and the thing of dread that he was completing. Even yet, we knew, a delay of minutes might doom irretrievably our own world and this interlocking one.

Abruptly I was aroused from these gloomy musings by a wild shout on one of the airboats just behind our own, and as I stared about I saw swooping down upon our fleet from high above, a dozen or more of the great flying-platforms, that had evidently been scouting high above us and were now plunging straight toward us. For the moment there was only wild confusion in the bird-men's fleet as their ancient enemies flashed down upon them, and that moment was used with a deadly advantage by the spider-men above. For as they drove down upon us, shaft upon shaft of the brilliant orange rays was searing down to cut lengthwise along our fleet, sending a score of our ships into instant annihilation before we could recover from the shock of that staggering and deadly attack.

As the platforms whirled down above us and up again for another plunge, though, Nor-Kan cried out a sharp order, and from our own ship and the hundreds behind us, a hail of deadly missiles from the static-guns whizzed out toward the speeding platforms that had now drawn some distance ahead of us. So innumerable were the missiles fired, and so close was the distance, that before the platforms could flee, all but three of them were glowing with faint light as the shots struck them and charged them, and then from beneath, bolt upon bolt of shattering lightning had leapt up from the ground far beneath and struck the glowing platforms, in blasting bursts, of dazzling electrical fire, so that they whirled down in riven, blackened masses toward the ground.

THE three platforms, which had escaped the missiles, were racing northward away from us, now, at their highest velocity, in an attempt to escape, and up toward and after them leapt a score of the swiftest of our craft. We saw the orange rays of the three burn back and annihilate several of the pursuing boats, but as they disappeared in the distance ahead of us, we saw the static-guns hit their mark in two cases, at least, as two of the fleeing platforms were struck by the terrific lightning from beneath. Then the remaining platform and the pursuing airboats had vanished from sight, and when some minutes later the airboats returned, it was to report that the platform had escaped them, due to its start upon them, and had vanished while still heading toward the north.

"No surprise now!" exclaimed Nor-Kan grimly, as our great fleet leapt on. "We may get there, though, before the spider-men can gather their fleet!"

At the highest speed of which our ships were capable, we drove northward, now, for we knew that the escaping platform would spread the alarm instantly and bring down upon us all the overwhelming forces of the spider-men, from all their scores of cities. Our only chance to accomplish what we sought, was to reach the spider-city, which was our goal, before the enemy could assemble, and so now it was in a tense race against time that our thousand ships sped north. Faces set and tense, Nor-Kan and Rawlins and I stood on the flagship's deck, gazing away to the north while the blue plain far below unrolled with unvarying speed, and while the long files of ships behind us, their formation a mote compact one, now drove through the air on our tracks.

On we flashed, toward the north, while hour followed hour and while the sun climbed up to the zenith and was slipping down again. Then abruptly Rawlins raised his hand, with an exclamation, and pointed away toward the horizon ahead. We all gazed, with hearts suddenly beating more swiftly, and then Nor-Kan had turned, had given an order, calmly and quietly, and our whole great fleet was slanting up toward a still greater height. For there, far ahead of us, there hung in the haze above the horizon a long, wavering line of small black specks, specks that were rapidly growing larger, growing distinct in shape as square black platforms, as they rushed toward us. It was the spider-fleet!

On they came, in a long, curving line of length so great that its two out-curving horns could hold within them the whole mass of our own fleet. A full five thousand platforms must have been in that mighty line, we knew, and at the sight of such overpowering odds a closed hand seemed to hold my heart tightly. Then, as the two fleets rushed madly together, the despair that had gripped me vanished, and in a strange calm as if I had become an impersonal spectator, I watched the nearing swarms of platforms.

In a great semi-circle they were flashing toward us now, and as they came nearer, innumerable dazzling streaks of the brilliant molecular ray burned out from them, shafts of orange light that cut through the air toward our ships like questing fingers of death. I heard hoarse shouts about me now, saw ship after ship of our fleet vanishing as the slicing, whirling rays reached them, but before more of the platforms could fire upon us, Nor-Kan had snapped a quick order and as a signal flashed from our flagship our whole fleet veered sharply to one side, and instead of moving on between the out-curving horns of the spider-fleet's formation, which would have exposed us to the concentrated rays of all their platforms, we sped past the rim of the semi-circular formation, which screened us effectually from the rays of the greater part of their fleet.

As we flashed past the outer side of their formation thus, there leapt out from the massed static-guns of our airboats hundreds of the metal missiles, the majority of which struck the platforms they were aimed at, and the next moment while those platforms, glowing now with the static charge, leapt upward in an effort to escape, there flashed up from beneath them the destroying bolts. I heard a crazy cheer from the birdmen on the craft about me as our fleet, still holding its formation, wheeled quickly to speed back upon the spider-fleet's other side and repeat our maneuver, for literally scores of their platforms were whirling downward in flaming masses as a result of that skillful attack. Before we could repeat it, though, they had seen our intention, and as if in answer to an order, their formation abruptly broke up completely, and in a disorganized vast swarm of single platforms, they turned and leapt upon us.

It was a tactic, which we had not anticipated, and for the moment it took us at a complete loss. Before any order could be formulated to meet the change in the situation, the flying-platforms were rushing upon and among us, in compact groups, and then as their rays whirled about and cut great lanes of destruction among us, our own formation vanished and our ships sought individual opponents among the myriad platforms that were speeding upon and among them.

The next moment it seemed that our flagship was lost in a whirling, tossing sea of striking and struggling ships and platforms, a hell of battle raging about and above and beneath us, stunning to the senses. Out from the omnipresent groups of platforms streaked the deadly orange rays, whirling and stabbing, their effects not noticeable at once, except for the empty gaps that opened abruptly in the field of battle, where airboats had been but a moment before.

And from our ships in turn leaped the shining cartridges of the static-guns, platforms all about us glowing faintly as the missiles struck them, and bolt upon bolt of crashing lightning leaping up from the ground far beneath to strike those glowing platforms.

From all about us, it seemed, the orange rays were flashing toward our own ship, the flagship, and it was only the skill of the bird-man at the controls that saved us from annihilation in that mad moment. With tremendous speed our craft dipped and twisted to avoid the whirling rays, our own static-guns raining shining missiles upon the surrounding platforms, but even so one of the stabbing rays struck close enough above our decks to instantly decapitate a half-dozen of the bird-men at the static-guns. At once I sprang with Rawlins to the guns, and while Nor-Kan, as calmly as ever, shouted his orders behind us, we swung the guns upon the platforms that swooped and circled about and above us, and whose rays cut crazily through the masses of struggling ships.

I saw one of the big, square platforms leaping toward us from the right out of the ruck of the battle, and in that wild melee, I seemed to observe it with photographic clearness and accuracy in that instant, the cylindrical mechanism at its corner, the score of hideous, many-limbed spider-men crouched upon its surface, the ray-tubes along its sides, all microscopically clear before my eyes. Then as it flashed toward us and as I saw a spider-man upon it gripping his ray-tube and swing it full upon us, I swung the static-gun in my grasp straight toward him and before he could loose the ray, the missile from my gun had spread a glowing light over the platform and the crashing lightning-bolt from far below had smitten it and changed it into a fiery mass of fused metals and charred bodies that tumbled crazily downward.

As it did so, we were thrown violently to the deck, as our craft swerved sharply sidewise, just in time to escape a slender shaft of the brilliant orange ray, that grazed up past us and demolished a struggling airboat above us. In the next moment, the platform from below that had loosed that ray was struck by a blasting bolt from the ground as an airboat beside it struck it with one of the static-missiles. And then that airboat in turn had vanished, hit in that unguarded moment by a ray from its other side. As it did so I heard Rawlins cry out, point upward, and saw hovering directly above us one of the platforms that was swinging its ray-tubes down toward us. There was no time to swing up our own static guns, no time to swerve aside but the next moment the bird-man at the controls had jerked them sharply back and sent our airboat racing upward, its sharp prow striking the edge of the platform above and tipping the big flat square sharply over so that it swung clumsily in mid-air for an instant in that position. Then a shining missile had struck it and a crashing bolt from far beneath demolished it as our ship drove up above the battle.

UP we flashed, up until the field of the battle stretched a thousand feet below us, a mighty, far-flung mass of whirling platforms and airboats, of stabbing orange rays and lightning-flashes from beneath. Platform after platform had reeled down, struck by those tremendous bolts, but the tremendous disparity in numbers had told against us and now but a half or less of our original fleet struggled below us, against platforms many times their number. Such an unequal struggle could not last for long, I knew, but now I heard Nor-Kan utter a short order, and as a series of signals was flashed from our flagship, circling there above the battle, there flashed up to join us a dozen airboats which until then, by his orders, had taken no part in the struggle.

As they drove up beside us, I saw that these were the craft which the scientists of the bird-people had hastily equipped with a newly-devised weapon of which I knew nothing, a long, blunt black cylinder that was mounted at the prow of each airboat. They gathered about us, then turned the cylinders down upon the flying-platforms that were swarming in fierce attack upon our airboats there below. As they aimed the blunt cylinders, there came from them a loud humming, but no other evidence of operation. Looking down, though, I saw the platforms below at which they were aimed tumbling helplessly down toward the ground, far below, reeling down in crazy destruction toward the blue plains, while all about us the bird-men cheered madly. Over their shouting, Nor-Kan explained to me that the blunt cylinders were similar to the cylinder-mechanisms upon the platforms themselves, which propelled those platforms by giving them a powerful magnetic charge which caused them to be attracted by this world's magnetic poles. The blunt cylinders on our airboats, in turn, gave to the platforms at which they were aimed an equal charge of opposite polarity, and the two thus equalizing each other, the platforms were attracted by neither pole and robbed of their sustaining and propelling powers, tumbled down to destruction on the ground far below.

Platform after platform was falling now, while from our airboats below the static-guns were vomiting a rain of deadly missiles upon the spider-men who still opposed them. Swiftly the odds were changing, and now it seemed that within a few minutes more the battle would be over, since but a scant few hundred of the platforms were left. Abruptly, however, these massed together, seemed to pause for an instant. Then we saw a group of the spider-men massing around a small globular apparatus on one of the platforms, and even as we turned our weapons upon these massed platforms, even as the airboats below leapt toward them, we learned the reason for action, and learned that they too had weapons of which we knew nothing. For before either our magnetic cylinders or the static-guns of the airboats below could be trained upon them, all light about us suddenly vanished, plunging us into a rayless night, in which there gleamed no single spark of light!

From all around us and from far below, we could hear cries of dismay and fear from the bird-men on our airboats, as the blazing white sunlight about them gave way in an instant to that impenetrable darkness. The nature of that darkness was plain enough; it was obviously produced by some apparatus of the spider-men which killed the vibrations of light by opposing to them a dampening vibration, extinguishing every ray of light over an unguessed area. Blindly we drifted through that torturing darkness, and from below we could hear shattering crashes as our airboats collided with one another in that darkness. Then I felt a wind on my face as our craft began to move swiftly through the darkness, at an order from Nor-Kan, and a moment later it burst abruptly out of the darkness into the fierce white light of day.

Behind us lay the dark area, like a vast blot of blackness in the heavens, produced by the apparatus on the platform that must still have hovered at its center, but now we saw that the other platforms, no more than a few hundred in number, had taken advantage of the concealing darkness they had thrown about them to flee, since away to the northward their dark shapes could be seen diminishing as they sped from us. Our own airboats were gropingly emerging from that lightless area, now, and as they gathered about us again. Nor-Kan shouted an order and we raced northward after the fleeing platforms, only a score of our own ships remaining and firing static-missiles into that dark area in an effort to destroy the platform with the apparatus which produced it, inside. As we sped away, I saw the blackness suddenly vanish, and knew that their missiles had found the lurking platform inside it, and then they were speeding along with us in hot pursuit of the flying shapes in the distance.

On we flashed, a fleet still over five hundred strong, while far ahead of us the remaining scores of platforms fled. "They're making for their city—the city where we were!" Rawlins shouted in my ear, over the roar of the wind that was about us now as we raced on. "They must know that Adams is almost ready to transpose their cities and them, into our world!"

I nodded mutely, my eyes upon the dark, flashing shapes ahead, and I saw, beyond them, the looming, gigantic cones of the spider-city where we had been imprisoned. The dark, mighty cones, the tremendous wall about them, the cables that led from the top of the cones to each other, all were as they had been, though now those cables and the streets beneath were swarming with innumerable hordes of the spider-creatures, racing about in wildest confusion as their shattered fleet drove down toward them. And down after that fleet our own ships flashed, down until we were within hundreds of feet of the tops of the mighty cones, down until we could see the clearing at the city's center, and in it the single cone, and upon that cone's top a single dark figure who was working madly with the connections of a great mass of apparatus before him.

"*Adams!*" shouted Rawlins, pointing downward, and I too shouted as I saw what was happening, saw that now, at the last moment, Adams was struggling to complete the last details of the controls which would in a moment transpose all the mighty city around him, and all its hordes, and all the other hordes and cities of the spider-men, into our interlocking world. Down toward that central cone our whole fleet swooped, but up to protect it there rose the last few hundred ships of the spider-men's fleet, the last few hundred platforms that came crazily up toward us in a last wild effort to hold us back from that building-top below where Adams was working madly to complete the connections of the apparatus that would give to them another world.

Up they came toward us, and the next moment we had met them and over the city of the spider-men there was swift, terrific battle, orange ray and static-missile leaping from airboat to platform and from platform to airboat, craft of bird-men and spider-creatures alike smashing down to death in the city below them. Above the top of the central cone there hung the last of the platforms, resisting with the mad energy of despair all our efforts to reach it. All about us airboats and platforms alike were reeling and falling and vanishing, amid the fury of that wild combat, but now, one by one, the platforms were being annihilated, and now as a gap opened between them, Nor-Kan, at the controls of, our own airboat, sent it whirling down toward the top of the great cone below us.

As our airboat swooped downward, the rays of the platforms on either side swept along it, annihilating the last of our bird-men crew and leaving only Nor-Kan beside Rawlins and myself. In a moment more the craft had crashed down at the edge of the cone-top, where Adams, oblivious to the battle above, was working madly on the last of his connections. We sprang out upon the building's top, but as we did so, there poured up on the ascending belt-stairway a half-dozen of the spider-men, leaping between us and Adams. I saw Nor-Kan strike out in great blows that sent two to the floor, and then, as Rawlins and I were gripped by others, saw him lift one bodily and hurl him down into the round shaft up which the ascending belt moved, down through the building toward its floor far beneath. Then he too was struggling with the remaining one. While Rawlins and I twisted in the grip of our opponents with the madness of utter despair.

I glimpsed Adams, burning-eyed, finishing his connections, saw that the last of the platforms were almost gone, that the airboats were swooping down toward us. In that moment, though, there came a crazy shout from Adams, and he was leaping toward the metal pillar that rose from the floor just beside the shaft of the ascending belt, was leaping toward the big lever-switch upon that pillar from which ran the connections of all the massed apparatus behind him, the connections, I knew, of all the great ray-projectors in all the cities of the spider-men, I saw his hand close upon that switch, as I struggled helplessly in the grip of my spider-man opponent, and knew that the next instant would see the closing of that switch, the turning on of the projected ray at full force on the city around us and on all the cities of the spider-men, the transposition of all those cities, all those hordes, into the world of man, never to be undone.

But in that moment there came a hoarse shout from Rawlins where he struggled with his own opponent by the roof's edge, and I saw him hurl the hideous figure of that opponent from him with superhuman force breaking him bodily upon the floor, saw him leap forward toward Adams, toward the switch. As he leaped, Adams saw him. Jerked down the switch with a swift motion, down the graduated slot, which measured the force of the ray, it loosed. But he was late—an instant late. For as he jerked it down, Rawlins' hand had shot up toward it, had stopped it half-way down the slot, so that instead of the ray's full force, it loosed upon the spider-cities but half that force.

THERE was an instant of utter silence and stillness, an instant in which it seemed that all motion and all sound in all the world had ceased. Then there broke about us a titanic detonation that was like the crash of meeting spheres, the death-shout of riven worlds. And in that instant the vast city about us, the massed gigantic cones and the cables that connected them, and the streets below and all the spider-hordes in the streets and on cables, all these had vanished, disappeared, whiffed out of existence, so that about this central cone there now lay nothing but a vast depression in the barren blue soil, the city that had stood for ages upon it was gone.

Gone! Gone forever; gone as all the cities and all the hordes of the spider-creatures were gone, whiffed into sheer non-existence when the ray that was to have transposed them into our world, was turned on at half-force instead of full-force, not having power enough to reverse the motions of the electrons, in the interlocking masses of matter, to transpose them from world to world, having power enough only to halt those motions, to destroy that matter as though it had never been. In our own world, I knew, the corresponding sections of matter that interlocked with the spider-cities must have been annihilated at the same moment, but what was that small loss compared to the doom of man's world that had been prevented? What was it compared to the removal forever of the menace of the spider-creatures from the two locked worlds?

As that tremendous detonation died away, Nor-Kan and I had almost at the same moment, thrust from us our opponents, limp and dead, and now we leaped forward to where Rawlins and Adams struggled by the switch. But before we could reach them, we saw Adams thrust Rawlins back, saw him gaze around, a hell of hate in his burning eyes as he saw his work thus destroyed, his vast and evil plans thus thwarted. Then he had whipped one of the deadly ray-tubes from his belt, leveled it upon us, stepping sidewise to loose that death in a sweeping circle upon us. But as he did so, as he stepped unseeingly, his foot encountered empty space—the open belt-shaft beside the switch—and he reeled down into that shaft, only a thin scream coming up toward us as he whirled downward, and then a dull, half-heard thudding sound from far beneath.

We stood motionless, all but senseless, and then saw that the last of the platforms had been annihilated, that the airboats were swooping down upon us, down upon the top of our cone, the last left of all the vanished city. We stepped to our own airboat, and began driving up with the others, up above the cone-top, up until all hovered motionless high over it. Then a rain of shining missiles swept down upon it, the great structure glowed everywhere with faint light, and then from all about it there had leapt crashing bolts of terrific lightning, mighty electrical discharges, that wreathed the great cone for an instant in a shroud of violet fire. Then it had crumbled, crashed, fallen, and as the dust-cloud of its collapse cleared away from the place where it had stood, we saw that only a low mound of shattered, blackened fragments lay there, the last of the works of the spider-creatures, of all their hordes and cities. Then, as we hung there, we became suddenly conscious that in all the world at that moment there reigned, a tremendous silence.

CHAPTER SIX

IT was days later that Rawlins and I, standing in the little crater where first we had found ourselves in this strange world, bade our friends, the bird-people farewell. Those days following the destruction of the spider-creatures and their cities, we had spent in the polar land of the bird-men, and there, with the help of their scientists, we had constructed a transposition-apparatus like that by which we had come into this interlocking world from our own. Now, standing there in the hot white sunlight at the little crater's bottom, with the big disk-apparatus behind us, we faced the scores of bird-men who had come north again with us to this spot to see us go.

One by one, in their deep tones, they wished us well and tried to express their gratitude for what we had done for them, assuring us that when we had gone, the transposition-apparatus would be destroyed, and the last link between the two interlocking worlds on their side would be severed. One by one we took our leave of them, there in the brilliant light of the blue-white sun above, and then last of all of them, Nor-Kan came forward, his face strangely still and solemn, and gripped with his taloned hands, the hands which we outstretched toward him; he stood thus for a moment in silence.

"Goodbye, Rawlins—Harker," he said. "We are different far, bird-man and human, but we have fought and dared together, at least. And together we have helped to save our worlds."

We wrung his taloned hands, without speaking, and then turned toward the big disk-apparatus behind us, the masses of apparatus to which it was connected. Slowly we stepped upon the lower disk, and then, more slowly still, Rawlins reached out toward the switch. He grasped it and then, even as we had done before, we paused, glancing around for a last time at the weird, wild landscape that we should never behold again. Nor-Kan and the other bird-men gathered about us in the dazzling white sunlight, on the blue ground studded with shining pebbles, with the slowly moving patches of blue vegetation. Then Rawlins jerked down the switch.

Again, from the disk above us, a blinding white light poured down upon us, and as it flooded through us with the same titanic force, I had a last glimpse of the weird landscape revolving about me with immense speed, and then it had vanished, as we seemed to be sucked down into a roaring maelstrom of darkness, on which I involuntarily closed my eyes. The roaring lessened, the wild motion that had thrilled me died, and slowly I opened my eyes again. And, even as I had expected, I found myself with Rawlins beside me in his little laboratory, its electric lights still burning and its door still tightly locked.

Beside us there stood the big disk-apparatus by which we had gone into the Interlocking world after Adams, and in a moment we had dismantled it, had smashed its delicate actuating apparatus with heavy blows, had closed forever the last gate between the two interlocking worlds, the two universes, a gate that was never meant for man or any other to open or pass through. Then we left the little laboratory, the big building, and paused outside on its steps.

It was night in the world outside, as when we had left it, a softly scented summer night in which the only sounds were a few distant voices, and the whispering of the breeze. We had no thought, in that moment, for the strange wonder that would be stirring this world concerning the cataclysms that had blasted it out of the unknown, had no desire to explain to that world how through those cataclysms had it and the world locked with it been saved from a dreadful doom. We wanted only to stand there, in that moment, silent, motionless, with the cool wind upon our faces, and the soft, familiar sound of human voices in our ears, and above our heads the calm, unchanging splendor of the stars.

THE END

If you've enjoyed this book, you will not want to miss these terrific titles…

ARMCHAIR SCI-FI & HORROR DOUBLE NOVELS, $12.95 each

D-11   **PERIL OF THE STARMEN** by Kris Neville
           THE STRANGE INVASION by Murray Leinster

D-12   **THE STAR LORD** by Boyd Ellanby
           CAPTIVES OF THE FLAME by Samuel R. Delany

D-13   **MEN OF THE MORNING STAR** by Edmond Hamilton
           PLANET FOR PLUNDER by Hal Clement and Sam Merwin, Jr.

D-14   **ICE CITY OF THE GORGON** by Chester S. Geier and Richard Shaver
           WHEN THE WORLD TOTTERED by Lester del Rey

D-15   **WORLDS WITHOUT END** by Clifford D. Simak
           THE LAVENDER VINE OF DEATH by Don Wilcox

D-16   **SHADOW ON THE MOON** by Joe Gibson
           ARMAGEDDON EARTH by Geoff St. Reynard

D-17   **THE GIRL WHO LOVED DEATH** by Paul W. Fairman
           SLAVE PLANET by Laurence M. Janifer

D-18   **SECOND CHANCE** by J. F. Bone
           MISSION TO A DISTANT STAR by Frank Belknap Long

D-19   **THE SYNDIC** by C. M. Kornbluth
           FLIGHT TO FOREVER by Poul Anderson

D-20   **SOMEWHERE I'LL FIND YOU** by Milton Lesser
           THE TIME ARMADA by Fox B. Holden

ARMCHAIR SCIENCE FICTION CLASSICS, $12.95 each

C-4   **CORPUS EARTHLING**
          by Louis Charbonneau

C-5   **THE TIME DISSOLVER**
          by Jerry Sohl

C-6   **WEST OF THE SUN**
          by Edgar Pangborn

ARMCHAIR SCI-FI & HORROR GEMS SERIES, $12.95 each

G-1   **SCIENCE FICTION GEMS, Vol. One**
          Isaac Asimov and others

G-2   **HORROR GEMS, Vol. One**
          Carl Jacobi and others

If you've enjoyed this book, you will not want to miss these terrific titles…

ARMCHAIR SCI-FI & HORROR DOUBLE NOVELS, $12.95 each

D-21   **EMPIRE OF EVIL** by Robert Arnette
THE SIGN OF THE TIGER by Alan E. Nourse & J. A. Meyer

D-22   **OPERATION SQUARE PEG** by Frank Belknap Long
ENCHANTRESS OF VENUS by Leigh Brackett

D-23   **THE LIFE WATCH** by Lester del Rey
CREATURES OF THE ABYSS by Murray Leinster

D-24   **LEGION OF LAZARUS** by Edmond Hamilton
STAR HUNTER by Andre Norton

D-25   **EMPIRE OF WOMEN** by John Fletcher
ONE OF OUR CITIES IS MISSING by Irving Cox

D-26   **THE WRONG SIDE OF PARADISE** by Raymond F. Jones
THE INVOLUNTARY IMMORTALS by Rog Phillips

D-27   **EARTH QUARTER** by Damon Knight
ENVOY TO NEW WORLDS by Keith Laumer

D-28   **SLAVES TO THE METAL HORDE** by Milton Lesser
HUNTERS OUT OF TIME by Joseph E. Kelleam

D-29   **RX JUPITER SAVE US** by Ward Moore
BEWARE THE USURPERS by Geoff St. Reynard

D-30   **SECRET OF THE SERPENT** by Don Wilcox
CRUSADE ACROSS THE VOID by Dwight V. Swain

ARMCHAIR SCIENCE FICTION CLASSICS, $12.95 each

C-7   **THE SHAVER MYSTERY, Book One**
by Richard S. Shaver

C-8   **THE SHAVER MYSTERY, Book Two**
by Richard S. Shaver

C-9   **MURDER IN SPACE**
by David V. Reed

ARMCHAIR MASTERS OF SCIENCE FICTION SERIES, $16.95 each

M-3   **MASTERS OF SCIENCE FICTION, Vol. Three**
Robert Sheckley, "The Perfect Woman" and other tales

M-4   **MASTERS OF SCIENCE FICTION, Vol. Four**
Mack Reynolds, Part One, "Stowaway" and other tales

If you've enjoyed this book, you will not want to miss these terrific titles…

ARMCHAIR SCI-FI & HORROR DOUBLE NOVELS, $12.95 each

D-31 **A HOAX IN TIME** by Keith Laumer
INSIDE EARTH by Poul Anderson

D-32 **TERROR STATION** by Dwight V. Swain
THE WEAPON FROM ETERNITY by Dwight V. Swain

D-33 **THE SHIP FROM INFINITY** by Edmond Hamilton
TAKEOFF by C. M. Kornbluth

D-34 **THE METAL DOOM** by David H. Keller
TWELVE TIMES ZERO by Howard Browne

D-35 **HUNTERS OUT OF SPACE** by Joseph Kelleam
INVASION FROM THE DEEP by Paul W. Fairman,

D-36 **THE BEES OF DEATH** by Robert Moore Williams
A PLAGUE OF PYTHONS by Frederik Pohl

D-37 **THE LORDS OF QUARMALL** by Fritz Leiber and Harry Fischer
BEACON TO ELSEWHERE by James H. Schmitz

D-38 **BEYOND PLUTO** by John S. Campbell
ARTERY OF FIRE by Thomas N. Scortia

D-39 **SPECIAL DELIVERY** by Kris Neville
NO TIME FOR TOFFEE by Charles F. Meyers

D-40 **JUNGLE IN THE SKY** by Milton Lesser
RECALLED TO LIFE by Robert Silverberg

ARMCHAIR SCIENCE FICTION CLASSICS, $12.95 each

C-10 **MARS IS MY DESTINATION**
by Frank Belknap Long

C-11 **SPACE PLAGUE**
by George O. Smith

C-12 **SO SHALL YE REAP**
by Rog Phillips

ARMCHAIR SCI-FI & HORROR GEMS SERIES, $12.95 each

G-3 **SCIENCE FICTION GEMS, Vol. Two**
James Blish and others

G-4 **HORROR GEMS, Vol. Two**
Joseph Payne Brennan and others

If you've enjoyed this book, you will not want to miss these terrific titles…

ARMCHAIR SCI-FI & HORROR DOUBLE NOVELS, $12.95 each

D-41   **FULL CYCLE** by Clifford D. Simak
            IT WAS THE DAY OF THE ROBOT by Frank Belknap Long

D-42   **THIS CROWDED EARTH** by Robert Bloch
            REIGN OF THE TELEPUPPETS by Daniel Galouye

D-43   **THE CRISPIN AFFAIR** by Jack Sharkey
            THE RED HELL OF JUPITER by Paul Ernst

D-44   **PLANET OF DREAD** by Dwight V. Swain
            WE THE MACHINE by Gerald Vance

D-45   **THE STAR HUNTER** by Edmond Hamilton
            THE ALIEN by Raymond F. Jones

D-46   **WORLD OF IF** by Rog Phillips
            SLAVE RAIDERS FROM MERCURY by Don Wilcox

D-47   **THE ULTIMATE PERIL** by Robert Abernathy
            PLANET OF SHAME by Bruce Elliot

D-48   **THE FLYING EYES** by J. Hunter Holly
            SOME FABULOUS YONDER by Phillip Jose Farmer

D-49   **THE COSMIC BUNGLERS** by Geoff St. Reynard
            THE BUTTONED SKY by Geoff St. Reynard

D-50   **TYRANTS OF TIME** by Milton Lesser
            PARIAH PLANET by Murray Leinster

ARMCHAIR SCIENCE FICTION CLASSICS, $12.95 each

C-13   **SUNKEN WORLD**
            by Stanton A. Coblentz

C-14   **THE LAST VIAL**
            by Sam McClatchie, M. D.

C-15   **WE WHO SURVIVED (THE FIFTH ICE AGE)**
            by Sterling Noel

ARMCHAIR MASTERS OF SCIENCE FICTION SERIES, $16.95 each

MS-5   **MASTERS OF SCIENCE FICTION, Vol. Five**
            Winston K. Marks—Test Colony and other tales

MS-6   **MASTERS OF SCIENCE FICTION, Vol. Six**
            Fritz Leiber—Deadly Moon and other tales

If you've enjoyed this book, you will not want to miss these terrific titles…

ARMCHAIR SCI-FI & HORROR DOUBLE NOVELS, $12.95 each

ARMCHAIR SCIENCE FICTION CLASSICS, $12.95 each

ARMCHAIR SCI-FI & HORROR GEMS SERIES, $12.95 each

MAROONED ON A LOST CONTINENT OF PREHISTORIC BEASTS!

Bowen Tyler's adventure began with a terror-haunted trip as a captive in an enemy submarine. It ended on the rocky shores of a lost world, an unmapped land forgotten by the rest of humanity, where the wild beasts and the beast-men of the Stone Age still lived and fought as they had hundreds of thousands of years ago.

What was the secret of this mysterious continent, where the march of time had apparently stopped and where giant dinosaurs, ferocious saber-tooth tigers, and savage ape-men still struggled for their lives with tooth and claw?

"The Land that Time Forgot" is an epic of imagination and science fiction adventure by one of the greatest science fiction authors of the Twentieth Century, Edgar Rice Burroughs—the man who gave us "A Princess of Mars."

ABOUT EDGAR RICE BURROUGHS:

Edgar Rice Burroughs was born in Chicago in 1875. He is universally acclaimed for his amazing novels of science fiction, fantasy, and adventure. He is best known for Tarzan's jungle adventures, the wilds of Pellucidar, and of course…John Carter's escapades on Mars.

Prior to his fame as a writer, Burroughs attempted a number of different careers, but he met with little success. Then at the age of 35 he turned to writing. He achieved instant success with the publication of his two best known novels, *A Princess of Mars* and *Tarzan of the Apes*.

During his career, he wrote nearly seventy novels spanning many different genres. He was also a mainstay in the pulp magazines of the '30s and '40s, often appearing in *Amazing Stories* and *Fantastic Adventures*. During World War Two, in spite of his advanced age, he also gained fame as a successful war correspondent.

Burroughs left a beloved legacy of brilliant stories, a product of his seemingly endless imagination. Edgar Rice Burroughs died in Tarzana, California on March 19th, 1950.

THE LAND
THAT TIME
FORGOT

By
EDGAR RICE BURROUGHS

ARMCHAIR FICTION
PO Box 4369, Medford, Oregon 97501-0168

*For more information about Armchair Books and products, visit our
website at…*

www.armchairfiction.com

Or email us at…

armchairfiction@yahoo.com

CHAPTER ONE

It must have been a little after three o'clock in the afternoon that it happened—the afternoon of June 3rd, 1916. It seems incredible that all that I have passed through—all those weird and terrifying experiences—should have been encompassed within so short a span as three brief months. Rather might I have experienced a cosmic cycle, with all its changes and evolutions for that which I have seen with my own eyes in this brief interval of time—things that no other mortal eye had seen before, glimpses of a world past, a world dead, a world so long dead that even in the lowest Cambrian stratum no trace of it remains. Fused with the melting inner crust, it has passed forever beyond the ken of man other than in that lost pocket of the earth whither fate has borne me and where my doom is sealed. I am here and here must remain.

After reading this far, my interest, which already had been stimulated by the finding of the manuscript, was approaching the boiling-point. I had come to Greenland for the summer, on the advice of my physician, and was slowly being bored to extinction, as I had thoughtlessly neglected to bring sufficient reading-matter. Being an indifferent fisherman, my enthusiasm for this form of sport soon waned; yet in the absence of other forms of recreation I was now risking my life in an entirely inadequate boat off Cape Farewell at the southernmost extremity of Greenland.

Greenland! As a descriptive appellation, it is a sorry joke—but my story has nothing to do with Greenland, nothing to do with me; so I shall get through with the one and the other as rapidly as possible.

The inadequate boat finally arrived at a precarious landing, the natives, waist-deep in the surf, assisting. I was carried ashore, and while the evening meal was being prepared, I wandered to and fro along the rocky, shattered shore. Bits of surf-harried beach clove the worn granite, or whatever the rocks of Cape Farewell may be composed of, and as I followed the ebbing tide down one of these soft stretches, I saw the thing. Were one to bump into a Bengal tiger in the ravine behind the Bimini Baths, one could be no more surprised than was I to see a perfectly good quart thermos bottle turning and twisting in the surf of Cape Farewell at the southern extremity of Greenland. I rescued it, but I was soaked above the knees doing it; and then I sat down in the sand and opened it, and in the long twilight read the manuscript, neatly written and tightly folded, which was its contents.

You have read the opening paragraph, and if you are an imaginative idiot like myself, you will want to read the rest of it; so I shall give it to you here, omitting quotation marks—which are difficult of remembrance. In two minutes you will forget me.

My home is in Santa Monica. I am, or was, junior member of my father's firm. We are ship-builders. Of recent years we have specialized on submarines, which we have built for Germany, England, France and the United States. I know a sub as a mother knows her baby's face, and have commanded a score of them on their trial runs. Yet my inclinations were all toward aviation. I graduated under Curtiss, and after a long siege with my father obtained his permission to try for the Lafayette Escadrille. As a stepping-stone I obtained an appointment in the American ambulance service and was on my way to France when three shrill whistles altered, in as many seconds, my entire scheme of life.

I was sitting on deck with some of the fellows who were going into the American ambulance service with me, my Airedale, Crown Prince Nobbler, asleep at my feet, when the first blast of the whistle shattered the peace and security of the ship. Ever since entering the U-boat zone we had been on the lookout for periscopes, and children that we were, bemoaning the unkind fate that was to see us safely into France on the morrow without a glimpse of the dread marauders. We were young; we craved thrills, and God knows we got them that day; yet by comparison with that through which I have since passed they were as tame as a Punch-and-Judy show.

I shall never forget the ashy faces of the passengers as they stampeded for their life-belts, though there was no panic. Nobs rose with a low growl. I rose, also, and over the ship's side, I saw not two hundred yards distant the periscope of a submarine, while racing toward the liner the wake of a torpedo was distinctly visible. We were aboard an American ship—which, of course, was not armed. We were entirely defenseless; yet without warning, we were being torpedoed.

I stood rigid, spellbound, watching the white wake of the torpedo. It struck us on the starboard side almost amidships. The vessel rocked as though the sea beneath it had been uptorn by a mighty volcano. We were thrown to the decks, bruised and stunned, and then above the ship, carrying with it fragments of steel and wood and dismembered human bodies, rose a column of water hundreds of feet into the air.

The silence which followed the detonation of the exploding torpedo was almost equally horrifying. It lasted for perhaps two seconds, to be followed by the screams and moans of the wounded, the cursing of the men and the hoarse commands of the ship's officers. They were splendid—they and their crew. Never before had I been so proud of my nationality as I was that moment. In all the chaos which followed the torpedoing of the liner no officer or member of the crew lost his head or showed in the slightest any degree of panic or fear.

While we were attempting to lower boats, the submarine emerged and trained guns on us. The officer in command ordered us to lower our flag, but this the captain of the liner refused to do. The ship was listing frightfully to starboard, rendering the port boats useless, while half the starboard boats had been demolished by the explosion. Even while the passengers were crowding the starboard rail and scrambling into the few boats left to us, the submarine commenced shelling the ship. I saw one shell burst in a group of women and children, and then I turned my head and covered my eyes.

When I looked again to horror was added chagrin, for with the emerging of the U-boat I had recognized her as a product of our own shipyard. I knew her to a rivet. I had superintended her construction. I had sat in that very conning-tower and directed the efforts of the sweating crew below when first her prow clove the sunny summer waters of the Pacific; and now this creature of my brain and hand had turned Frankenstein, bent upon pursuing me to my death.

A second shell exploded upon the deck. One of the lifeboats, frightfully overcrowded, swung at a dangerous angle from its davits. A fragment of the shell shattered the bow tackle, and I saw the women and children and the men vomited into the sea beneath, while the boat dangled stern up for a moment from its single davit, and at last with increasing momentum dived into the midst of the struggling victims screaming upon the face of the waters.

Now I saw men spring to the rail and leap into the ocean. The deck was tilting to an impossible angle. Nobs braced himself with all four feet to keep from slipping into the scuppers and looked up into my face with a questioning whine. I stooped and stroked his head.

"Come on, boy!" I cried, and running to the side of the ship, dived headforemost over the rail. When I came up, the first thing I saw was Nobs swimming about in a bewildered sort of way a few yards from me. At sight of me his ears went flat, and his lips parted in a characteristic grin.

The submarine was withdrawing toward the north, but all the time it was shelling the open boats, three of them, loaded to the gunwales with survivors. Fortunately the small boats presented a rather poor target, which, combined with the bad marksmanship of the Germans preserved their occupants from harm; and after a few minutes a blotch of smoke appeared upon the eastern horizon and the U-boat submerged and disappeared.

All the time the lifeboats had been pulling away from the danger of the sinking liner, and now, though I yelled at the top of my lungs, they either did not hear my appeals for help or else did not dare return to succor me. Nobs and I had gained some little distance from the ship when it rolled completely over and sank. We were caught in the suction only enough to be drawn backward a few yards, neither of us being carried beneath the surface. I glanced hurriedly about for something to which to cling. My eyes were directed toward the point at which the liner had disappeared when there came from the depths of the ocean the muffled reverberation of an explosion, and almost simultaneously a geyser of water in which were shattered lifeboats, human bodies, steam, coal, oil, and the flotsam of a liner's deck leaped high above the surface of the sea—a watery column momentarily marking the grave of another ship in this greatest cemetery of the seas.

When the turbulent waters had somewhat subsided and the sea had ceased to spew up wreckage, I ventured to swim back in search of something substantial enough to support my weight and that of Nobs as well. I had gotten well over the area of the wreck when not a half-dozen yards ahead of me a lifeboat shot bow foremost out of the ocean almost its entire length to flop down upon its keel with a mighty splash. It must have been carried far below, held to its mother ship by a single rope which finally parted to the enormous strain put upon it. In no other way can I account for its having leaped so far out of the water—a beneficent circumstance to which I doubtless owe my life, and that of another far dearer to me than my own. I say beneficent circumstance even in the face of the fact that a fate far more hideous confronts us than that which we escaped that day; for because of that circumstance I have met her whom otherwise I never should have known; I have met and loved her. At least I have had that great happiness in life; nor can Caspak, with all her horrors, expunge that which has been.

So for the thousandth time I thank the strange fate which sent that lifeboat hurtling upward from the green pit of destruction to which it had been dragged—sent it far up above the surface, emptying its water as it rose above the waves, and dropping it upon the surface of the sea, buoyant and safe.

It did not take me long to clamber over its side and drag Nobs in to comparative safety, and then I glanced around upon the scene of death and desolation which surrounded us. The sea was littered with wreckage among which floated the pitiful forms of women and children, buoyed up by their useless lifebelts. Some were torn and mangled; others lay rolling quietly to the motion of the sea, their countenances composed and peaceful; others were set in hideous lines of agony or horror. Close to the boat's side floated the figure of a girl. Her face was turned upward, held above the surface by her life-belt, and was framed in a floating mass of dark and waving hair. She was very beautiful. I had never looked upon such perfect features, such a divine molding which was at the same time human—intensely human. It was a face filled with character and strength and femininity—the face of one who was created to love and to be loved. The cheeks were flushed to the hue of life and health and vitality, and yet she lay there upon the bosom of the sea, dead. I felt something rise in my throat as I looked down upon that radiant vision, and I swore that I should live to avenge her murder.

And then I let my eyes drop once more to the face upon the water, and what I saw nearly tumbled me backward into the sea, for the eyes in the dead face had opened; the lips had parted; and one hand was raised toward me in a mute appeal for succor. She lived! She was not dead! I leaned over the boat's side and drew her quickly in to the comparative safety which God had given me. I removed her life-belt and my soggy coat and made a pillow for her head. I chafed her hands and arms and feet. I worked over her for an hour, and at last I was rewarded by a deep sigh, and again those great eyes opened and looked into mine.

At that I was all embarrassment. I have never been a ladies' man; at Leland-Stanford I was the butt of the class because of my hopeless imbecility in the presence of a pretty girl; but the men liked me, nevertheless. I was rubbing one of her hands when she opened her eyes, and I dropped it as though it were a red-hot rivet. Those eyes took me in slowly from head to foot; then they wandered slowly around the horizon marked by the rising and falling gunwales of the lifeboat. They looked at Nobs and softened, and then came back to me filled with questioning.

"I—I—" I stammered, moving away and stumbling over the next thwart. The vision smiled wanly.

"Aye-aye, sir!" she replied faintly, and again her lips drooped, and her long lashes swept the firm, fair texture of her skin.

"I hope that you are feeling better," I finally managed to say.

"Do you know," she said after a moment of silence, "I have been awake for a long time! But I did not dare open my eyes. I thought I must be dead, and I was afraid to look, for fear that I should see nothing but blackness about me. I am afraid to die! Tell me what happened after the ship went down. I remember all that happened before—oh, but I wish that I might forget it!" A sob broke her voice. "The beasts!" she went on after a moment. "And to think that I was to have married one of them—a lieutenant in the German navy."

Presently she resumed as though she had not ceased speaking. "I went down and down and down. I thought I should never cease to sink. I felt no particular distress until I suddenly started upward at ever-increasing velocity; then my lungs seemed about to burst, and I must have lost consciousness, for I remember nothing more until I opened my eyes after listening to a torrent of invective against Germany and Germans. Tell me, please, all that happened after the ship sank."

I told her, then, as well as I could, all that I had seen—the submarine shelling the open boats and all the rest of it. She thought it marvelous that we should have been spared in so providential a manner, and I had a pretty speech upon my tongue's end, but lacked the nerve to deliver it. Nobs had come over and nosed his muzzle into her lap, and she stroked his ugly face, and at last she leaned over and put her cheek against his forehead. I have always admired Nobs; but this was the first time that it had ever occurred to me that I might wish to be Nobs. I wondered how he would take it, for he is as unused to women as I. But he took to it as a duck takes to water. What I lack of being a ladies' man, Nobs certainly makes up for as a ladies' dog. The old scalawag just closed his eyes and put on one of the softest "sugar-wouldn't-melt-in-my-mouth" expressions you ever saw and stood there taking it and asking for more. It made me jealous.

"You seem fond of dogs," I said.

"I am fond of this dog," she replied.

Whether she meant anything personal in that reply I did not know; but I took it as personal and it made me feel mighty good.

As we drifted about upon that vast expanse of loneliness it is not strange that we should quickly become well acquainted. Constantly we scanned the horizon for signs of smoke, venturing guesses as to our chances of rescue; but darkness settled, and the black night enveloped us without ever the sight of a speck upon the waters.

We were thirsty, hungry, uncomfortable, and cold. Our wet garments had dried but little and I knew that the girl must be in grave danger from the exposure to a night of cold and wet upon the water in an open boat, without sufficient clothing and no food. I had managed to bail all the water out of the boat with cupped hands, ending by mopping the balance up with my handkerchief—a slow and back-breaking procedure; thus I had made a comparatively dry place for the girl to lie down low in the bottom of the boat, where the sides would protect her from the night wind, and when at last she did so, almost overcome as she was by weakness and fatigue, I threw my wet coat over her further to thwart the chill. But it was of no avail; as I sat watching her, the moonlight marking out the graceful curves of her slender young body, I saw her shiver.

"Isn't there something I can do?" I asked. "You can't lie there chilled through all night. Can't you suggest something?"

She shook her head. "We must grin and bear it," she replied after a moment.

Nobbler came and lay down on the thwart beside me, his back against my leg, and I sat staring in dumb misery at the girl, knowing in my heart of hearts that she might die before morning came, for what with the shock and exposure, she had already gone through enough to kill almost any woman. And as I gazed down at her, so small and delicate and helpless, there was born slowly within my breast a new emotion. It had never been there before; now it will never cease to be there. It made me almost frantic in my desire to find some way to keep warm and cooling lifeblood in her veins. I was cold myself, though I had almost forgotten it until Nobbler moved and I felt a new sensation of cold along my leg against which he had lain, and suddenly realized that in that one spot I had been warm. Like a great light came the understanding of a means to warm the girl. Immediately I knelt beside her to put my scheme into practice when suddenly I was overwhelmed with embarrassment. Would she permit it, even if I could somehow muster the courage to suggest it? Then I saw her entire frame convulse, shudderingly, her muscles reacting to her rapidly lowering temperature, and casting prudery to the winds, I threw myself down beside her and took her in my arms, pressing her body close to mine.

She drew away suddenly, voicing a little cry of fright, and tried to push me from her.

"Forgive me," I managed to stammer. "It is the only way. You will die of exposure if you are not warmed, and Nobs and I are the only means we can command for furnishing warmth." And I held her tightly while I called Nobs and bade him lie down at her back. The girl didn't struggle any more when she learned my purpose; but she gave two or three little gasps, and then began to cry softly, burying her face on my arm, and thus she fell asleep.

CHAPTER TWO

Toward morning, I must have dozed, though it seemed to me at the time that I had lain awake for days, instead of hours. When I finally opened my eyes, it was daylight, and the girl's hair was in my face, and she was breathing normally. I thanked God for that. She had turned her head during the night so that as I opened my eyes I saw her face not an inch from mine, my lips almost touching hers.

It was Nobs who finally awoke her. He got up, stretched, turned around a few times and lay down again, and the girl opened her eyes and looked into mine. Hers went very wide at first, and then slowly comprehension came to her, and she smiled.

"You have been very good to me," she said, as I helped her to rise, though if the truth were known I was more in need of assistance than she; the circulation all along my left side seeming to be paralyzed entirely. "You have been very good to me." And that was the only mention she ever made of it; yet I know that she was thankful and that only reserve prevented her from referring to what, to say the least, was an embarrassing situation, however unavoidable.

Shortly after daylight we saw smoke apparently coming straight toward us, and after a time we made out the squat lines of a tug—one of those fearless exponents of England's supremacy of the sea that tows sailing ships into French and English ports. I stood up on a thwart and waved my soggy coat above my head. Nobs stood upon another and barked. The girl sat at my feet straining her eyes toward the deck of the oncoming boat. "They see us," she said at last. "There is a man answering your signal." She was right. A lump came into my throat—for her sake rather than for mine. She was saved, and none too soon. She could not have lived through another night upon the Channel; she might not have lived through the coming day.

The tug came close beside us, and a man on deck threw us a rope. Willing hands dragged us to the deck, Nobs scrambling nimbly aboard without assistance. The rough men were gentle as mothers with the girl. Plying us both with questions they hustled her to the captain's cabin and me to the boiler-room. They told the girl to take off her wet clothes and throw them outside the door that they might be dried, and then to slip into the captain's bunk and get warm. They didn't have to tell me to strip after I once got into the warmth of the boiler-room. In a jiffy, my clothes hung about where they might dry most quickly, and I myself was absorbing, through every pore, the welcome heat of the stifling compartment. They brought us hot soup and coffee, and then those who were not on duty sat around and helped me damn the Kaiser and his brood.

As soon as our clothes were dry, they bade us don them, as the chances were always more than fair in those waters that we should run into trouble with the enemy, as I was only too well aware. What with the warmth and the feeling of safety for the girl, and the knowledge that a little rest and food would quickly overcome the effects of her experiences of the past dismal hours, I was feeling more content than I had experienced since those three whistle-blasts had shattered the peace of my world the previous afternoon.

But peace upon the Channel has been but a transitory thing since August, 1914. It proved itself such that morning, for I had scarce gotten into my dry clothes and taken the girl's apparel to the captain's cabin when an order was shouted down into the engine-room for full speed ahead, and an instant later I heard the dull boom of a gun. In a moment

I was up on deck to see an enemy submarine about two hundred yards off our port bow. She had signaled us to stop, and our skipper had ignored the order; but now she had her gun trained on us, and the second shot grazed the cabin, warning the belligerent tug-captain that it was time to obey. Once again an order went down to the engine-room, and the tug reduced speed. The U-boat ceased firing and ordered the tug to come about and approach. Our momentum had carried us a little beyond the enemy craft, but we were turning now on the arc of a circle that would bring us alongside her. As I stood watching the maneuver and wondering what was to become of us, I felt something touch my elbow and turned to see the girl standing at my side. She looked up into my face with a rueful expression. "They seem bent on our destruction," she said, "and it looks like the same boat that sunk us yesterday."

"It is," I replied. "I know her well. I helped design her and took her out on her first run."

The girl drew back from me with a little exclamation of surprise and disappointment. "I thought you were an American," she said. "I had no idea you were a—a—"

"Nor am I," I replied. "Americans have been building submarines for all nations for many years. I wish, though, that we had gone bankrupt, my father and I, before ever we turned out that Frankenstein of a thing."

We were approaching the U-boat at half speed now, and I could almost distinguish the features of the men upon her deck. A sailor stepped to my side and slipped something hard and cold into my hand. I did not have to look at it to know that it was a heavy pistol. "Tyke 'er an' use 'er," was all he said.

Our bow was pointed straight toward the U-boat now as I heard word passed to the engine for full speed ahead. I instantly grasped the brazen effrontery of the plucky English skipper—he was going to ram five hundreds tons of U-boat in the face of her trained gun. I could scarce repress a cheer. At first the boches didn't seem to grasp his intention. Evidently they thought they were witnessing an exhibition of poor seamanship, and they yelled their warnings to the tug to reduce speed and throw the helm hard to port.

We were within fifty feet of them when they awakened to the intentional menace of our maneuver. Their gun crew was off its guard; but they sprang to their piece now and sent a futile shell above our heads. Nobs leaped about and barked furiously. "Let 'em have it!" commanded the tug-captain, and instantly revolvers and rifles poured bullets upon the deck of the submersible. Two of the gun-crew went down; the other trained their piece at the water-line of the oncoming tug. The balance of those on deck replied to our small-arms fire, directing their efforts toward the man at our wheel.

I hastily pushed the girl down the companionway leading to the engine-room, and then I raised my pistol and fired my first shot at a boche. What happened in the next few seconds happened so quickly that details are rather blurred in my memory. I saw the helmsman lunge forward upon the wheel, pulling the helm around so that the tug sheered off quickly from her course, and I recall realizing that all our efforts were to be in vain, because of all the men aboard, Fate had decreed that this one should fall first to an enemy bullet. I saw the depleted gun-crew on the submarine fire their piece and I felt the shock of impact and heard the loud explosion as the shell struck and exploded in our bows.

I saw and realized these things even as I was leaping into the pilot-house and grasping the wheel, standing astride the dead body of the helmsman. With all my strength I threw the helm to starboard; but it was too late to effect the purpose of our skipper. The best I did was to scrape alongside the sub. I heard someone shriek an order into the engine-room; the boat shuddered and trembled to the sudden reversing of the engines, and our speed quickly lessened. Then I saw what that madman of a skipper planned since his first scheme had gone wrong.

With a loud-yelled command, he leaped to the slippery deck of the submersible, and at his heels came his hardy crew. I sprang from the pilot-house and followed, not to be left out in the cold when it came to strafing the boches. From the engine room companionway came the engineer and stockers, and together we leaped after the balance of the crew and into the hand-to-hand fight that was covering the wet deck with red blood. Beside me came Nobs, silent now, and grim. Germans were emerging from the open hatch to take part in the battle on deck. At first the pistols cracked amidst the cursing of the men and the loud commands of the commander and his junior; but presently we were too indiscriminately mixed to make it safe to use our firearms, and the battle resolved itself into a hand-to-hand struggle for possession of the deck.

The sole aim of each of us was to hurl one of the opposing force into the sea. I shall never forget the hideous expression upon the face of the great Prussian with whom chance confronted me. He lowered his head and rushed at me, bellowing like a bull. With a quick side-step and ducking low beneath his outstretched arms, I eluded him; and as he turned to come back at me, I landed a blow upon his chin which sent him spinning toward the edge of the deck. I saw his wild endeavors to regain his equilibrium; I saw him reel drunkenly for an instant upon the brink of eternity and then, with a loud scream, slip into the sea. At the same instant a pair of giant arms encircled me from behind and lifted me entirely off my feet. Kick and squirm as I would, I could neither turn toward my antagonist nor free myself from his maniacal grasp. Relentlessly he was rushing me toward the side of the vessel and death. There was none to stay him, for each of my companions was more than occupied by from one to three of the enemy. For an instant I was fearful for myself, and then I saw that which filled me with a far greater terror for another.

My boche was bearing me toward the side of the submarine against which the tug was still pounding. That I should be ground to death between the two was lost upon me as I saw the girl standing alone upon the tug's deck, as I saw the stern high in air and the bow rapidly settling for the final dive, as I saw death from which I could not save her clutching at the skirts of the woman I now knew all too well that I loved.

I had perhaps the fraction of a second longer to live when I heard an angry growl behind us mingle with a cry of pain and rage from the giant who carried me. Instantly he went backward to the deck, and as he did so he threw his arms outwards to save himself, freeing me. I fell heavily upon him, but was upon my feet in the instant. As I arose, I cast a single glance at my opponent. Never again would he menace me or another, for Nob's great jaws had closed upon his throat. Then I sprang toward the edge of the deck closest to the girl upon the sinking tug.

"Jump!" I cried. "Jump!" And I held out my arms to her. Instantly as though with implicit confidence in my ability to save her, she leaped over the side of the tug onto the sloping, slippery side of the U-boat. I reached far over to seize her hand. At the same instant the tug pointed its stern straight toward the sky and plunged out of sight. My hand missed the girl's by a fraction of an inch, and I saw her slip into the sea; but scarce had she touched the water when I was in after her.

The sinking tug drew us far below the surface; but I had seized her the moment I struck the water, and so we went down together, and together we came up—a few yards from the U-boat. The first thing I heard was Nobs barking furiously; evidently he had missed me and was searching. A single glance at the vessel's deck assured me that the battle was over and that we had been victorious, for I saw our survivors holding a handful of the enemy at pistol points while one by one the rest of the crew was coming out of the craft's interior and lining up on deck with the other prisoners.

As I swam toward the submarine with the girl, Nobs' persistent barking attracted the attention of some of the tug's crew, so that as soon as we reached the side there were hands to help us aboard. I asked the girl if she was hurt, but she assured me that she was none the worse for this second wetting; nor did she seem to suffer any from shock. I was to learn for myself that this slender and seemingly delicate creature possessed the heart and courage of a warrior.

As we joined our own party, I found the tug's mate checking up our survivors. There were ten of us left, not including the girl. Our brave skipper was missing, as were eight others. There had been nineteen of us in the attacking party and we had accounted in one way and another during the battle for sixteen Germans and had taken nine prisoners, including the commander. His lieutenant had been killed.

"Not a bad day's work," said Bradley, the mate, when he had completed his roll. "Only losing the skipper," he added, "was the worst. He was a fine man, a fine man."

Olson—who in spite of his name was Irish, and in spite of his not being Scotch had been the tug's engineer—was standing with Bradley and me. "Yis," he agreed, "it's a day's wor-rk we're after doin', but what are we goin' to be doin' wid it now we got it?"

"We'll run her into the nearest English port," said Bradley, "and then we'll all go ashore and get our V.C.'s," he concluded, laughing.

"How you goin' to run her?" queried Olson. "You can't trust these Dutchmen."

Bradley scratched his head. "I guess you're right," he admitted. "And I don't know the first thing about a sub."

"I do," I assured him. "I know more about this particular sub than the officer who commanded her."

Both men looked at me in astonishment, and then I had to explain all over again as I had explained to the girl. Bradley and Olson were delighted. Immediately I was put in command, and the first thing I did was to go below with Olson and inspect the craft thoroughly for hidden boches and damaged machinery. There were no Germans below, and everything was intact and in ship-shape working order. I then ordered all hands below except one man who was to act as lookout. Questioning the Germans, I found that all except the commander were willing to resume their posts and aid in bringing the vessel into an English port. I believe that they were relieved at the prospect of being detained at a comfortable English prison-camp for the duration of the war after the perils and privations through which they had passed. The officer, however, assured me that he would never be a party to the capture of his vessel.

There was, therefore, nothing to do but put the man in irons. As we were preparing to put this decision into force, the girl descended from the deck. It was the first time that she or the German officer had seen each other's faces since we had boarded the U-boat. I was assisting the girl down the ladder and still retained a hold upon her arm—possibly after such support was no longer necessary—when she turned and looked squarely into the face of the German. Each voiced a sudden exclamation of surprise and dismay.

"Lys!" he cried, and took a step toward her.

The girl's eyes went wide, and slowly filled with a great horror, as she shrank back. Then her slender figure stiffened to the erectness of a soldier, and with chin in air and without a word she turned her back upon the officer.

"Take him away," I directed the two men who guarded him, "and put him in irons."

When he had gone, the girl raised her eyes to mine. "He is the German of whom I spoke," she said. "He is Baron von Schoenvorts."

I merely inclined my head. She had loved him! I wondered if in her heart of hearts she did not love him yet. Immediately I became insanely jealous. I hated Baron Friedrich von Schoenvorts with such utter intensity that the emotion thrilled me with a species of exaltation.

But I didn't have much chance to enjoy my hatred then, for almost immediately the lookout poked his face over the hatchway and bawled down that there was smoke on the horizon, dead ahead. Immediately I went on deck to investigate, and Bradley came with me.

"If she's friendly," he said, "we'll speak her. If she's not, we'll sink her—eh, captain?"

"Yes, lieutenant," I replied, and it was his turn to smile.

We hoisted the Union Jack and remained on deck, asking Bradley to go below and assign to each member of the crew his duty, placing one Englishman with a pistol beside each German.

"Half speed ahead," I commanded.

More rapidly now we closed the distance between ourselves and the stranger, until I could plainly see the red ensign of the British merchant marine. My heart swelled with pride at the thought that presently admiring British tars would be congratulating us upon our notable capture; and just about then the merchant steamer must have sighted us, for she veered suddenly toward the north, and a moment later dense volumes of smoke issued from her funnels. Then, steering a zigzag course, she fled from us as though we had been the bubonic plague. I altered the course of the submarine and set off in chase; but the steamer was faster than we, and soon left us hopelessly astern.

With a rueful smile, I directed that our original course be resumed, and once again we set off toward merry England. That was three months ago, and we haven't arrived yet; nor is there any likelihood that we ever shall.

The steamer we had just sighted must have wirelessed a warning, for it wasn't half an hour before we saw more smoke on the horizon, and this time the vessel flew the white ensign of the Royal Navy and carried guns. She didn't veer to the north or anywhere else, but bore down on us rapidly. I was just preparing to signal her, when a flame flashed from her bows, and an instant later the water in front of us was thrown high by the explosion of a shell.

Bradley had come on deck and was standing beside me. "About one more of those, and she'll have our range," he said. "She doesn't seem to take much stock in our Union Jack."

A second shell passed over us, and then I gave the command to change our direction, at the same time directing Bradley to go below and give the order to submerge. I passed Nobs down to him, and following, saw to the closing and fastening of the hatch.

It seemed to me that the diving-tanks never had filled so slowly. We heard a loud explosion apparently directly above us; the craft trembled to the shock which threw us all to the deck. I expected momentarily to feel the deluge of inrushing water, but none came. Instead we continued to submerge until the manometer registered forty feet and then I knew that we were safe. Safe! I almost smiled. I had relieved Olson, who had remained in the tower at my direction, having been a member of one of the early British submarine crews, and therefore having some knowledge of the business. Bradley was at my side. He looked at me quizzically.

"What the devil are we to do?" he asked. "The merchantman will flee us; the war-vessel will destroy us; neither will believe our colors or give us a chance to explain. We will meet even a worse reception if we go nosing around a British port—mines, nets and all of it. We can't do it."

"Let's try it again when this fellow has lost the scent," I urged. "There must come a ship that will believe us."

And try it again we did, only to be almost rammed by a huge freighter. Later we were fired upon by a destroyer, and two merchantmen turned and fled at our approach. For two days we cruised up and down the Channel trying to tell some one, who would listen, that we were friends; but no one would listen. After our encounter with the first warship I had given instructions that a wireless message be sent out explaining our predicament; but to my chagrin I discovered that both sending and receiving instruments had disappeared.

"There is only one place you can go," von Schoenvorts sent word to me, "and that is Kiel. You can't land anywhere else in these waters. If you wish, I will take you there, and I can promise that you will be treated well."

"There is another place we can go," I sent back my reply, "and we will before we'll go to Germany. That place is hell."

CHAPTER THREE

Those were anxious days, during which I had but little opportunity to associate with Lys. I had given her the commander's room, Bradley and I taking that of the deck-officer, while Olson and two of our best men occupied the room ordinarily allotted to petty officers. I made Nobs' bed down in Lys' room, for I knew she would feel less alone.

Nothing of much moment occurred for a while after we left British waters behind us. We ran steadily along upon the surface, making good time. The first two boats we sighted made off as fast as they could go; and the third, a huge freighter, fired on us, forcing us to submerge. It was after this that our troubles commenced. One of the Diesel engines broke down in the morning, and while we were working on it, the forward port diving-tank commenced to fill. I was on deck at the time and noted the gradual list. Guessing at once what was happening, I leaped for the hatch and slamming it closed above my head, dropped to the centrale. By this time the craft was going down by the head with a most unpleasant list to port, and I didn't wait to transmit orders to some one else but ran as fast as I could for the valve that let the sea into the forward port diving-tank. It was wide open. To close it and to have the pump started that would empty it were the work of but a minute; but we had had a close call.

I knew that the valve had never opened itself. Some one had opened it—some one who was willing to die himself if he might at the same time encompass the death of all of us.

After that I kept a guard pacing the length of the narrow craft. We worked upon the engine all that day and night and half the following day. Most of the time we drifted idly upon the surface, but toward noon we sighted smoke due west, and having found that only enemies inhabited the world for us, I ordered that the other engine be started so that we could move out of the path of the oncoming steamer. The moment the engine started to turn, however, there was a grinding sound of tortured steel, and when it had been stopped, we found that some one had placed a cold-chisel in one of the gears.

It was another two days before we were ready to limp along, half repaired. The night before the repairs were completed, the sentry came to my room and awoke me. He was rather an intelligent fellow of the English middle class, in whom I had much confidence.

"Well, Wilson," I asked. "What's the matter now?"

He raised his finger to his lips and came closer to me. "I think I've found out who's doin' the mischief," he whispered, and nodded his head toward the girl's room. "I seen her sneakin' from the crew's room just now," he went on. "She'd been in gassin' wit' the boche commander. Benson seen her in there las' night, too, but he never said nothin' till I goes on watch tonight. Benson's sorter slow in the head, an' he never puts two an' two together till some one else has made four out of it."

If the man had come in and struck me suddenly in the face, I could have been no more surprised.

"Say nothing of this to anyone," I ordered. "Keep your eyes and ears open and report every suspicious thing you see or hear."

The man saluted and left me; but for an hour or more I tossed, restless, upon my hard bunk in an agony of jealousy and fear. Finally I fell into a troubled sleep. It was daylight when I awoke. We were steaming along slowly upon the surface, my orders having been to proceed at half speed until we could take an observation and determine our position.

The sky had been overcast all the previous day and all night; but as I stepped into the centrale that morning I was delighted to see that the sun was again shining. The spirits of the men seemed improved; everything seemed propitious. I forgot at once the cruel misgivings of the past night as I set to work to take my observations.

What a blow awaited me! The sextant and chronometer had both been broken beyond repair, and they had been broken just this very night. They had been broken upon the night that Lys had been seen talking with von Schoenvorts. I think that it was this last thought which hurt me the worst. I could look the other disaster in the face with equanimity; but the bald fact that Lys might be a traitor appalled me.

I called Bradley and Olson on deck and told them what had happened, but for the life of me I couldn't bring myself to repeat what Wilson had reported to me the previous night. In fact, as I had given the matter thought, it seemed incredible that the girl could have passed through my room, in which Bradley and I slept, and then carried on a conversation in the crew's room, in which Von Schoenvorts was kept, without having been seen by more than a single man.

Bradley shook his head. "I can't make it out," he said. "One of those boches must be pretty clever to come it over us all like this; but they haven't harmed us as much as they think; there are still the extra instruments."

It was my turn now to shake a doleful head. "There are no extra instruments," I told them. "They too have disappeared as did the wireless apparatus."

Both men looked at me in amazement. "We still have the compass and the sun," said Olson. "They may be after getting the compass some night; but they's too many of us around in the daytime fer 'em to get the sun."

It was then that one of the men stuck his head up through the hatchway and seeing me, asked permission to come on deck and get a breath of fresh air. I recognized him as Benson, the man who, Wilson had said, reported having seen Lys with von Schoenvorts two nights before. I motioned him on deck and then called him to one side, asking if he had seen anything out of the way or unusual during his trick on watch the night before. The fellow scratched his head a moment and said, "No," and then as though it was an afterthought, he told me that he had seen the girl in the crew's room about midnight talking with the German commander, but as there hadn't seemed to him to be any harm in that, he hadn't said anything about it. Telling him never to fail to report to me anything in the slightest out of the ordinary routine of the ship, I dismissed him.

Several of the other men now asked permission to come on deck, and soon all but those actually engaged in some necessary duty were standing around smoking and talking, all in the best of spirits. I took advantage of the absence of the men upon the deck to go below for my breakfast, which the cook was already preparing upon the electric stove. Lys, followed by Nobs, appeared as I entered the centrale. She met me with a pleasant "Good morning!" which I am afraid I replied to in a tone that was rather constrained and surly.

"Will you breakfast with me?" I suddenly asked the girl, determined to commence a probe of my own along the lines which duty demanded.

She nodded a sweet acceptance of my invitation, and together we sat down at the little table of the officers' mess.

"You slept well last night?" I asked.

"All night," she replied. "I am a splendid sleeper."

Her manner was so straightforward and honest that I could not bring myself to believe in her duplicity; yet— Thinking to surprise her into a betrayal of her guilt, I blurted out: "The chronometer and sextant were both destroyed last night; there is a traitor among us." But she never turned a hair by way of evidencing guilty knowledge of the catastrophe.

"Who could it have been?" she cried. "The Germans would be crazy to do it, for their lives are as much at stake as ours."

"Men are often glad to die for an ideal—an ideal of patriotism, perhaps," I replied; "and a willingness to martyr themselves includes a willingness to sacrifice others, even those who love them. Women are much the same, except that they will go even further than most men—they will sacrifice everything, even honor, for love."

I watched her face carefully as I spoke, and I thought that I detected a very faint flush mounting her cheek. Seeing an opening and an advantage, I sought to follow it up.

"Take von Schoenvorts, for instance," I continued: "he would doubtless be glad to die and take us all with him, could he prevent in no other way the falling of his vessel into enemy hands. He would sacrifice anyone, even you; and if you still love him, you might be his ready tool. Do you understand me?"

She looked at me in wide-eyed consternation for a moment, and then she went very white and rose from her seat. "I do," she replied, and turning her back upon me, she walked quickly toward her room. I started to follow, for even believing what I did, I was sorry that I had hurt her. I reached the door to the crew's room just behind her and in time to see von Schoenvorts lean forward and whisper something to her as she passed; but she must have guessed that she might be watched, for she passed on.

That afternoon it clouded over; the wind mounted to a gale, and the sea rose until the craft was wallowing and rolling frightfully. Nearly everyone aboard was sick; the air became foul and oppressive. For twenty-four hours I did not leave my post in the conning tower, as both Olson and Bradley were sick. Finally I found that I must get a little rest, and so I looked about for some one to relieve me. Benson volunteered. He had not been sick, and assured me that he was a former R.N. man and had been detailed for submarine duty for over two years. I was glad that it was he, for I had considerable confidence in his loyalty, and so it was with a feeling of security that I went below and lay down.

I slept twelve hours straight, and when I awoke and discovered what I had done, I lost no time in getting to the conning tower. There sat Benson as wide awake as could be, and the compass showed that we were heading straight into the west. The storm was still raging; nor did it abate its fury until the fourth day. We were all pretty well done up and looked forward to the time when we could go on deck and fill our lungs with fresh air. During the whole four days I had not seen the girl, as she evidently kept closely to her room; and during this time no untoward incident had occurred aboard the boat—a fact which seemed to strengthen the web of circumstantial evidence about her.

For six more days after the storm lessened we still had fairly rough weather; nor did the sun once show himself during all that time. For the season—it was now the middle of June—the storm was unusual; but being from southern California, I was accustomed to unusual weather. In fact, I have discovered that the world over, unusual weather prevails at all times of the year.

We kept steadily to our westward course, and as the *U-33* was one of the fastest submersibles we had ever turned out, I knew that we must be pretty close to the North American coast. What puzzled me most was the fact that for six days we had not sighted a single ship. It seemed remarkable that we could cross the Atlantic almost to the coast of the

American continent without glimpsing smoke or sail, and at last I came to the conclusion that we were way off our course, but whether to the north or to the south of it I could not determine.

On the seventh day the sea lay comparatively calm at early dawn. There was a slight haze upon the ocean which had cut off our view of the stars; but conditions all pointed toward a clear morrow, and I was on deck anxiously awaiting the rising of the sun. My eyes were glued upon the impenetrable mist astern, for there in the east I should see the first glow of the rising sun that would assure me we were still upon the right course. Gradually the heavens lightened; but astern I could see no intenser glow that would indicate the rising sun behind the mist. Bradley was standing at my side. Presently he touched my arm.

"Look, captain," he said, and pointed south.

I looked and gasped, for there directly to port I saw outlined through the haze the red top of the rising sun. Hurrying to the tower, I looked at the compass. It showed that we were holding steadily upon our westward course. Either the sun was rising in the south, or the compass had been tampered with. The conclusion was obvious.

I went back to Bradley and told him what I had discovered. "And," I concluded, "we can't make another five hundred knots without oil; our provisions are running low and so is our water. God only knows how far south we have run."

"There is nothing to do," he replied, "other than to alter our course once more toward the west; we must raise land soon or we shall all be lost."

I told him to do so; and then I set to work improvising a crude sextant with which we finally took our bearings in a rough and most unsatisfactory manner; for when the work was done, we did not know how far from the truth the result might be. It showed us to be about 20° north and 30° west—nearly twenty-five hundred miles off our course. In short, if our reading was anywhere near correct, we must have been traveling due south for six days. Bradley now relieved Benson, for we had arranged our shifts so that the latter and Olson now divided the nights, while Bradley and I alternated with one another during the days.

I questioned both Olson and Benson closely in the matter of the compass; but each stoutly maintained that no one had tampered with it during his tour of duty. Benson gave me a knowing smile, as much as to say: "Well, you and I know who did this." Yet I could not believe that it was the girl.

We kept to our westerly course for several hours when the lookout's cry announced a sail. I ordered the *U-33*'s course altered, and we bore down upon the stranger, for I had come to a decision which was the result of necessity. We could not lie there in the middle of the Atlantic and starve to death if there was any way out of it. The sailing ship saw us while we were still a long way off, as was evidenced by her efforts to escape. There was scarcely any wind, however, and her case was hopeless; so when we drew near and signaled her to stop, she came into the wind and lay there with her sails flapping idly. We moved in quite close to her. She was the *Balmen* of Halmstad, Sweden, with a general cargo from Brazil for Spain.

I explained our circumstances to her skipper and asked for food, water and oil; but when he found that we were not German, he became very angry and abusive and started to draw away from us; but I was in no mood for any such business. Turning toward Bradley, who was in the conning-tower, I snapped out: "Gun-service on deck! To the diving stations!" We had no opportunity for drill; but every man had been posted as to his duties, and the German members of the crew understood that it was obedience or death for them, as each was accompanied by a man with a pistol. Most of them, though, were only too glad to obey me.

Bradley passed the order down into the ship and a moment later the gun-crew clambered up the narrow ladder and at my direction trained their piece upon the slow-moving Swede. "Fire a shot across her bow," I instructed the gun-captain.

Accept it from me, it didn't take that Swede long to see the error of his way and get the red and white pennant signifying "I understand" to the masthead. Once again the sails flapped idly, and then I ordered him to lower a boat and come after me. With Olson and a couple of the Englishmen I boarded the ship, and from her cargo selected what we needed—oil, provisions and water. I gave the master of the Balmen a receipt for what we took, together with an affidavit signed by Bradley, Olson, and myself, stating briefly how we had come into possession of the *U-33* and the urgency of our need for what we took. We addressed both to any British agent with the request that the owners of the Balmen be reimbursed; but whether or not they were, I do not know.[1]

With water, food, and oil aboard, we felt that we had obtained a new lease of life. Now, too, we knew definitely where we were, and I determined to make for Georgetown, British Guiana—but I was destined to again suffer bitter disappointment.

Six of us of the loyal crew had come on deck either to serve the gun or board the Swede during our set-to with her; and now, one by one, we descended the ladder into the centrale. I was the last to come, and when I reached the bottom, I found myself looking into the muzzle of a pistol in the hands of Baron Friedrich von Schoenvorts—I saw all my men lined up at one side with the remaining eight Germans standing guard over them.

I couldn't imagine how it had happened; but it had. Later I learned that they had first overpowered Benson, who was asleep in his bunk, and taken his pistol from him, and then had found it an easy matter to disarm the cook and the remaining two Englishmen below. After that it had been comparatively simple to stand at the foot of the ladder and arrest each individual as he descended.

The first thing von Schoenvorts did was to send for me and announce that as a pirate I was to be shot early the next morning. Then he explained that the U-33 would cruise in these waters for a time, sinking neutral and enemy shipping indiscriminately, and looking for one of the German raiders that was supposed to be in these parts.

He didn't shoot me the next morning as he had promised, and it has never been clear to me why he postponed the execution of my sentence. Instead he kept me ironed just as he had been; then he kicked Bradley out of my room and took it all to himself.

We cruised for a long time, sinking many vessels, all but one by gunfire, but we did not come across a German raider. I was surprised to note that von Schoenvorts often permitted Benson to take command; but I reconciled this by the fact that Benson appeared to know more of the duties of a submarine commander than did any of the stupid Germans.

Once or twice Lys passed me; but for the most part she kept to her room. The first time she hesitated as though she wished to speak to me; but I did not raise my head, and finally she passed on. Then one day came the word that we were about to round the Horn and that von Schoenvorts had taken it into his fool head to cruise up along the Pacific coast of North America and prey upon all sorts and conditions of merchantmen.

"I'll put the fear of God and the Kaiser into them," he said.

The very first day we entered the South Pacific we had an adventure. It turned out to be quite the most exciting adventure I had ever encountered. It fell about this way. About eight bells of the forenoon watch I heard a hail from the deck, and presently the footsteps of the entire ship's company, from the amount of noise I heard at the ladder. Some one yelled back to those who had not yet reached the level of the deck: "It's the raider, the German raider *Geier!*"

I saw that we had reached the end of our rope. Below all was quiet—not a man remained. A door opened at the end of the narrow hull, and presently Nobs came trotting up to me. He licked my face and rolled over on his back, reaching for me with his big, awkward paws. Then other footsteps sounded, approaching me. I knew whose they were, and I looked straight down at the flooring. The girl was coming almost at a run—she was at my side immediately. "Here!" she cried. "Quick!" And she slipped something into my hand. It was a key—the key to my irons. At my side she also laid a pistol, and then she went on into the centrale. As she passed me, I saw that she carried another pistol for herself. It did not take me long to liberate myself, and then I was at her side. "How can I thank you?" I started; but she shut me up with a word.

"Do not thank me," she said coldly. "I do not care to hear your thanks or any other expression from you. Do not stand there looking at me. I have given you a chance to do something—now do it!" The last was a peremptory command that made me jump.

Glancing up, I saw that the tower was empty, and I lost no time in clambering up, looking about me. About a hundred yards off lay a small, swift cruiser-raider, and above her floated the German man-of-war's flag. A boat had just been lowered, and I could see it moving toward us filled with officers and men. The cruiser lay dead ahead. "My," I thought, "what a wonderful targ—" I stopped even thinking, so surprised and shocked was I by the boldness of my imagery. The girl was just below me. I looked down on her wistfully. Could I trust her? Why had she released me at this moment? I must! I must! There was no other way. I dropped back below. "Ask Olson to step down here, please," I requested; "and don't let anyone see you ask him."

She looked at me with a puzzled expression on her face for the barest fraction of a second, and then she turned and went up the ladder. A moment later Olson returned, and the girl followed him. "Quick!" I whispered to the big Irishman, and made for the bow compartment where the torpedo-tubes are built into the boat; here, too, were the torpedoes. The girl accompanied us, and when she saw the thing I had in mind, she stepped forward and lent a hand to the swinging of the great cylinder of death and destruction into the mouth of its tube. With oil and main strength we shoved the torpedo home and shut the tube; then I ran back to the conning-tower, praying in my heart of hearts that the *U-33* had not swung her bow away from the prey. No, thank God!

Never could aim have been truer. I signaled back to Olson: "Let 'er go!" The *U-33* trembled from stem to stern as the torpedo shot from its tube. I saw the white wake leap from her bow straight toward the enemy cruiser. A chorus of hoarse yells arose from the deck of our own craft: I saw the officers stand suddenly erect in the boat that was approaching us, and I heard loud cries and curses from the raider. Then I turned my attention to my own business. Most of the men on the submarine's deck were standing in paralyzed fascination, staring at the torpedo. Bradley happened to be looking toward the conning-tower and saw me. I sprang on deck and ran toward him. "Quick!" I whispered. "While they are stunned, we must overcome them."

A German was standing near Bradley—just in front of him. The Englishman struck the fellow a frantic blow upon the neck and at the same time snatched his pistol from its holster. Von Schoenvorts had recovered from his first surprise quickly and had turned toward the main hatch to investigate. I covered him with my revolver, and at the same instant the torpedo struck the raider, the terrific explosion drowning the German's command to his men.

Bradley was now running from one to another of our men, and though some of the Germans saw and heard him, they seemed too stunned for action.

Olson was below, so that there were only nine of us against eight Germans, for the man Bradley had struck still lay upon the deck. Only two of us were armed; but the heart seemed to have gone out of the boches, and they put up but half-hearted resistance. Von Schoenvorts was the worst—he was fairly frenzied with rage and chagrin, and he came charging for me like a mad bull, and as he came he discharged his pistol. If he'd stopped long enough to take aim, he might have gotten me; but his pace made him wild, so that not a shot touched me, and then we clinched and went to the deck. This left two pistols, which two of my own men were quick to appropriate. The Baron was no match for me in a hand-to-hand encounter, and I soon had him pinned to the deck and the life almost choked out of him.

A half-hour later things had quieted down, and all was much the same as before the prisoners had revolted—only we kept a much closer watch on von Schoenvorts. The *Geier* had sunk while we were still battling upon our deck, and afterward we had drawn away toward the north, leaving the survivors to the attention of the single boat which had been making its way toward us when Olson launched the torpedo. I suppose the poor devils never reached land, and if they did, they most probably perished on that cold and unhospitable shore; but I couldn't permit them aboard the *U-33*. We had all the Germans we could take care of.

That evening the girl asked permission to go on deck. She said that she felt the effects of long confinement below, and I readily granted her request. I could not understand her, and I craved an opportunity to talk with her again in an effort to fathom her and her intentions, and so I made it a point to follow her up the ladder. It was a clear, cold, beautiful night. The sea was calm except for the white water at our bows and the two long radiating swells running far off into the distance upon either hand astern, forming a great V which our propellers filled with choppy waves. Benson was in the tower, we were bound for San Diego and all looked well.

Lys stood with a heavy blanket wrapped around her slender figure, and as I approached her, she half turned toward me to see who it was. When she recognized me, she immediately turned away.

"I want to thank you," I said, "for your bravery and loyalty—you were magnificent. I am sorry that you had reason before to think that I doubted you."

"You did doubt me," she replied in a level voice. "You practically accused me of aiding Baron von Schoenvorts. I can never forgive you."

There was a great deal of finality in both her words and tone.

"I could not believe it," I said; "and yet two of my men reported having seen you in conversation with von Schoenvorts late at night upon two separate occasions—after each of which some great damage was found done us in the morning. I didn't want to doubt you; but I carried all the responsibility of the lives of these men, of the safety of the ship, of your life and mine. I had to watch you, and I had to put you on your guard against a repetition of your madness."

She was looking at me now with those great eyes of hers, very wide and round.

"Who told you that I spoke with Baron von Schoenvorts at night, or any other time?" she asked.

"I cannot tell you, Lys," I replied, "but it came to me from two different sources."

"Then two men have lied," she asserted without heat. "I have not spoken to Baron von Schoenvorts other than in your presence when first we came aboard the *U-33*. And please, when you address me, remember that to others than my intimates I am Miss La Rue."

Did you ever get slapped in the face when you least expected it? No? Well, then you do not know how I felt at that moment. I could feel the hot, red flush surging up my neck, across my cheeks, over my ears, clear to my scalp. And it made me love her all the more; it made me swear inwardly a thousand solemn oaths that I would win her.

[1] Late in July, 1916, an item in the shipping news mentioned a Swedish sailing vessel, Balmen, Rio de Janeiro to Barcelona, sunk by a German raider sometime in June. A single survivor in an open boat was picked up off the Cape Verde Islands, in a dying condition. He expired without giving any details.

CHAPTER FOUR

For several days things went along in about the same course. I took our position every morning with my crude sextant; but the results were always most unsatisfactory. They always showed a considerable westing when I knew that we had been sailing due north. I blamed my crude instrument, and kept on. Then one afternoon the girl came to me.

"Pardon me," she said, "but were I you, I should watch this man Benson—especially when he is in charge." I asked her what she meant, thinking I could see the influence of von Schoenvorts raising a suspicion against one of my most trusted men.

"If you will note the boat's course a half-hour after Benson goes on duty," she said, "you will know what I mean, and you will understand why he prefers a night watch. Possibly, too, you will understand some other things that have taken place aboard."

Then she went back to her room, thus ending the conversation. I waited until half an hour after Benson had gone on duty, and then I went on deck, passing through the conning-tower where Benson sat, and looking at the compass. It showed that our course was north by west—that is, one point west of north, which was, for our assumed position, about right. I was greatly relieved to find that nothing was wrong, for the girl's words had caused me considerable apprehension. I was about to return to my room when a thought occurred to me that again caused me to change my mind—and, incidentally, came near proving my death-warrant.

When I had left the conning-tower little more than a half-hour since, the sea had been breaking over the port bow, and it seemed to me quite improbable that in so short a time an equally heavy sea could be deluging us from the opposite side of the ship—winds may change quickly, but not a long, heavy sea. There was only one other solution—since I left the tower, our course had been altered some eight points. Turning quickly, I climbed out upon the conning-tower. A single glance at the heavens confirmed my suspicions; the constellations which should have been dead ahead were directly starboard. We were sailing due west.

Just for an instant longer I stood there to check up my calculations—I wanted to be quite sure before I accused Benson of perfidy, and about the only thing I came near making quite sure of was death. I cannot see even now how I escaped it. I was standing on the edge of the conning-tower, when a heavy palm suddenly struck me between the shoulders and hurled me forward into space. The drop to the triangular deck forward of the conning-tower might easily have broken a leg for me, or I might have slipped off onto the deck and rolled overboard; but fate was upon my side, as I was only slightly bruised. As I came to my feet, I heard the conning-tower cover slam. There is a ladder which leads from the deck to the top of the tower. Up this I scrambled, as fast as I could go; but Benson had the cover tight before I reached it.

I stood there a moment in dumb consternation. What did the fellow intend? What was going on below? If Benson was a traitor, how could I know that there were not other traitors among us? I cursed myself for my folly in going out upon the deck, and then this thought suggested another—a hideous one: who was it that had really been responsible for my being here?

Thinking to attract attention from inside the craft, I again ran down the ladder and onto the small deck only to find that the steel covers of the conning-tower windows were shut, and then I leaned with my back against the tower and cursed myself for a gullible idiot.

I glanced at the bow. The sea seemed to be getting heavier, for every wave now washed completely over the lower deck. I watched them for a moment, and then a sudden chill pervaded my entire being. It was not the chill of wet clothing, or the dashing spray which drenched my face; no, it was the chill of the hand of death upon my heart. In an instant I had turned the last corner of life's highway and was looking God Almighty in the face—the *U-33* was being slowly submerged!

It would be difficult, even impossible, to set down in writing my sensations at that moment. All I can particularly recall is that I laughed, though neither from a spirit of bravado nor from hysteria. And I wanted to smoke. Lord! how I did want to smoke; but that was out of the question.

I watched the water rise until the little deck I stood on was awash, and then I clambered once more to the top of the conning-tower. From the very slow submergence of the boat I knew that Benson was doing the entire trick alone—that he was merely permitting the diving-tanks to fill and that the diving-rudders were not in use. The throbbing of the engines ceased, and in its stead came the steady vibration of the electric motors. The water was halfway up the conning-tower! I had perhaps five minutes longer on the deck. I tried to decide what I should do after I was washed away. Should I swim until exhaustion claimed me, or should I give up and end the agony at the first plunge?

From below came two muffled reports. They sounded not unlike shots. Was Benson meeting with resistance? Personally it could mean little to me, for even though my men might overcome the enemy, none would know of my predicament until long after it was too late to succor me. The top of the conning-tower was now awash. I clung to the wireless mast, while the great waves surged sometimes completely over me.

I knew the end was near and, almost involuntarily, I did that which I had not done since childhood—I prayed. After that I felt better.

I clung and waited, but the water rose no higher.

Instead it receded. Now the top of the conning-tower received only the crests of the higher waves; now the little triangular deck below became visible! What had occurred within? Did Benson believe me already gone, and was he emerging because of that belief, or had he and his forces been vanquished? The suspense was more wearing than that which I had endured while waiting for dissolution. Presently the main deck came into view, and then the conning-tower opened behind me, and I turned to look into the anxious face of Bradley. An expression of relief overspread his features.

"Thank God, man!" was all he said as he reached forth and dragged me into the tower. I was cold and numb and rather all in. Another few minutes would have done for me, I am sure, but the warmth of the interior helped to revive me, aided and abetted by some brandy which Bradley poured down my throat, from which it nearly removed the membrane. That brandy would have revived a corpse.

When I got down into the centrale, I saw the Germans lined up on one side with a couple of my men with pistols standing over them. Von Schoenvorts was among them. On the floor lay Benson, moaning, and beyond him stood the girl, a revolver in one hand. I looked about, bewildered.

"What has happened down here?" I asked. "Tell me!"

Bradley replied. "You see the result, sir," he said. "It might have been a very different result but for Miss La Rue.

We were all asleep. Benson had relieved the guard early in the evening; there was no one to watch him—no one but Miss La Rue. She felt the submergence of the boat and came out of her room to investigate. She was just in time to see Benson at the diving rudders. When he saw her, he raised his pistol and fired point-blank at her, but he missed and she fired—and didn't miss. The two shots awakened everyone, and as our men were armed, the result was inevitable as you see it; but it would have been very different had it not been for Miss La Rue. It was she who closed the diving-tank sea-cocks and roused Olson and me, and had the pumps started to empty them."

And there I had been thinking that through her machinations I had been lured to the deck and to my death! I could have gone on my knees to her and begged her forgiveness—or at least I could have, had I not been Anglo-Saxon. As it was, I could only remove my soggy cap and bow and mumble my appreciation. She made no reply—only turned and walked very rapidly toward her room. Could I have heard aright? Was it really a sob that came floating back to me through the narrow aisle of the *U-33*?

Benson died that night. He remained defiant almost to the last; but just before he went out, he motioned to me, and I leaned over to catch the faintly whispered words.

"I did it alone," he said. "I did it because I hate you—I hate all your kind. I was kicked out of your shipyard at Santa Monica. I was locked out of California. I am an I.W.W. I became a German agent—not because I love them, for I hate them too—but because I wanted to injure Americans, whom I hated more. I threw the wireless apparatus overboard. I destroyed the chronometer and the sextant. I devised a scheme for varying the compass to suit my wishes. I told Wilson that I had seen the girl talking with von Schoenvorts, and I made the poor egg think he had seen her doing the same thing. I am sorry—sorry that my plans failed. I hate you."

He didn't die for a half-hour after that; nor did he speak again—aloud; but just a few seconds before he went to meet his Maker, his lips moved in a faint whisper; and as I leaned closer to catch his words, what do you suppose I heard? "Now—I—lay me—down—to—sleep" That was all; Benson was dead. We threw his body overboard.

The wind of that night brought on some pretty rough weather with a lot of black clouds which persisted for several days. We didn't know what course we had been holding, and there was no way of finding out, as we could no longer trust the compass, not knowing what Benson had done to it. The long and the short of it was that we cruised about aimlessly until the sun came out again. I'll never forget that day or its surprises. We reckoned, or rather guessed, that we were somewhere off the coast of Peru. The wind, which had been blowing fitfully from the east, suddenly veered around into the south, and presently we felt a sudden chill.

"Peru!" snorted Olson. "When were yez after smellin' iceber-rgs off Peru?"

Icebergs! "Icebergs, nothin'!" exclaimed one of the Englishmen. "Why, man, they don't come north of fourteen here in these waters."

"Then," replied Olson, "ye're sout' of fourteen, me b'y."

We thought he was crazy; but he wasn't, for that afternoon we sighted a great berg south of us, and we'd been running north, we thought, for days. I can tell you we were a discouraged lot; but we got a faint thrill of hope early the next morning when the lookout bawled down the open hatch: "Land! Land northwest by west!"

I think we were all sick for the sight of land. I know that I was; but my interest was quickly dissipated by the sudden illness of three of the Germans. Almost simultaneously they commenced vomiting. They couldn't suggest any explanation for it. I asked them what they had eaten, and found they had eaten nothing other than the food cooked for all of us. "Have you drunk anything?" I asked, for I knew that there was liquor aboard, and medicines in the same locker.

"Only water," moaned one of them. "We all drank water together this morning. We opened a new tank. Maybe it was the water."

I started an investigation which revealed a terrifying condition—some one, probably Benson, had poisoned all the running water on the ship. It would have been worse, though, had land not been in sight. The sight of land filled us with renewed hope.

Our course had been altered, and we were rapidly approaching what appeared to be a precipitous headland. Cliffs, seemingly rising perpendicularly out of the sea, faded away into the mist upon either hand as we approached. The land before us might have been a continent, so mighty appeared the shoreline; yet we knew that we must be thousands of miles from the nearest western land-mass— New Zealand or Australia.

We took our bearings with our crude and inaccurate instruments; we searched the chart; we cudgeled our brains; and at last it was Bradley who suggested a solution. He was in the tower and watching the compass, to which he called my attention. The needle was pointing straight toward the land. Bradley swung the helm hard to starboard. I could feel the *U-33* respond, and yet the arrow still clung straight and sure toward the distant cliffs.

"What do you make of it?" I asked him.

"Did you ever hear of Caproni?" he asked.

"An early Italian navigator?" I returned.

"Yes; he followed Cook about 1721. He is scarcely mentioned even by contemporaneous historians—probably because he got into political difficulties on his return to Italy. It was the fashion to scoff at his claims, but I recall reading one of his works—his only one, I believe—in which he described a new continent in the south seas, a continent made up of 'some strange metal' which attracted the compass; a rockbound, inhospitable coast, without beach or harbor, which extended for hundreds of miles. He could make no landing; nor in the several days he cruised about it did he see sign of life. He called it Caprona and sailed away. I believe, sir, that we are looking upon the coast of Caprona, uncharted and forgotten for two hundred years."

"If you are right, it might account for much of the deviation of the compass during the past two days," I suggested. "Caprona has been luring us upon her deadly rocks. Well, we'll accept her challenge. We'll land upon Caprona. Along that long front there must be a vulnerable spot. We will find it, Bradley, for we must find it. We must find water on Caprona, or we must die."

And so we approached the coast upon which no living eyes had ever rested. Straight from the ocean's depths rose towering cliffs, shot with brown and blues and greens— withered moss and lichen and the verdigris of copper, and everywhere the rusty ocher of iron pyrites. The cliff-tops, though ragged, were of such uniform height as to suggest the boundaries of a great plateau, and now and again we caught glimpses of verdure topping the rocky escarpment, as though bush or jungle-land had pushed outward from a lush vegetation farther inland to signal to an unseeing world that Caprona lived and joyed in life beyond her austere and repellent coast.

But metaphor, however poetic, never slaked a dry throat. To enjoy Caprona's romantic suggestions we must have water, and so we came in close, always sounding, and skirted the shore. As close in as we dared cruise, we found fathomless depths, and always the same undented coastline of bald cliffs. As darkness threatened, we drew away and lay well off the coast all night. We had not as yet really commenced to suffer for lack of water; but I knew that it would not be long before we did, and so at the first streak of dawn I moved in again and once more took up the hopeless survey of the forbidding coast.

Toward noon we discovered a beach, the first we had seen. It was a narrow strip of sand at the base of a part of the cliff that seemed lower than any we had before scanned. At its foot, half buried in the sand, lay great boulders, mute evidence that in a bygone age some mighty natural force had crumpled Caprona's barrier at this point. It was Bradley who first called our attention to a strange object lying among the boulders above the surf.

"Looks like a man," he said, and passed his glasses to me.

I looked long and carefully and could have sworn that the thing I saw was the sprawled figure of a human being. Miss La Rue was on deck with us. I turned and asked her to go below. Without a word she did as I bade. Then I stripped, and as I did so, Nobs looked questioningly at me. He had been wont at home to enter the surf with me, and evidently he had not forgotten it.

"What are you going to do, sir?" asked Olson.

"I'm going to see what that thing is on shore," I replied. "If it's a man, it may mean that Caprona is inhabited, or it may merely mean that some poor devils were shipwrecked here. I ought to be able to tell from the clothing which is more near the truth."

"How about sharks?" queried Olson. "Sure, you ought to carry a knoife."

"Here you are, sir," cried one of the men.

It was a long slim blade he offered—one that I could carry between my teeth—and so I accepted it gladly.

"Keep close in," I directed Bradley, and then I dived over the side and struck out for the narrow beach. There was another splash directly behind me, and turning my head, I saw faithful old Nobs swimming valiantly in my wake.

The surf was not heavy, and there was no undertow, so we made shore easily, effecting an equally easy landing. The beach was composed largely of small stones worn smooth by the action of water. There was little sand, though from the deck of the *U-33* the beach had appeared to be all sand, and I saw no evidences of mollusca or crustacea such as are common to all beaches I have previously seen. I attribute this to the fact of the smallness of the beach, the enormous depth of surrounding water and the great distance at which Caprona lies from her nearest neighbor.

As Nobs and I approached the recumbent figure farther up the beach, I was appraised by my nose that whether or not, the thing had once been organic and alive, but that for some time it had been dead. Nobs halted, sniffed and growled. A little later he sat down upon his haunches, raised his muzzle to the heavens and bayed forth a most dismal howl. I shied a small stone at him and bade him shut up—his uncanny noise made me nervous. When I had come quite close to the thing, I still could not say whether it had been man or beast. The carcass was badly swollen and partly decomposed. There was no sign of clothing upon or about it. A fine, brownish hair covered the chest and abdomen, and the face, the palms of the hands, the feet, the shoulders and back were practically hairless. The creature must have been about the height of a fair sized man; its features were similar to those of a man; yet had it been a man?

I could not say, for it resembled an ape no more than it did a man. Its large toes protruded laterally as do those of the semiarboreal peoples of Borneo, the Philippines and other remote regions where low types still persist. The countenance might have been that of a cross between Pithecanthropus, the Java ape-man, and a daughter of the Piltdown race of prehistoric Sussex. A wooden cudgel lay beside the corpse.

Now this fact set me thinking. There was no wood of any description in sight. There was nothing about the beach to suggest a wrecked mariner. There was absolutely nothing about the body to suggest that it might possibly in life have known a maritime experience. It was the body of a low type of man or a high type of beast. In neither instance would it have been of a seafaring race. Therefore I deduced that it was native to Caprona—that it lived inland, and that it had fallen or been hurled from the cliffs above. Such being the case, Caprona was inhabitable, if not inhabited, by man; but how to reach the inhabitable interior! That was the question. A closer view of the cliffs than had been afforded me from the deck of the *U-33* only confirmed my conviction that no mortal man could scale those perpendicular heights; there was not a finger-hold, not a toe-hold, upon them. I turned away baffled.

Nobs and I met with no sharks upon our return journey to the submarine. My report filled everyone with theories and speculations, and with renewed hope and determination. They all reasoned along the same lines that I had reasoned— the conclusions were obvious, but not the water. We were now thirstier than ever.

The balance of that day we spent in continuing a minute and fruitless exploration of the monotonous coast. There was not another break in the frowning cliffs—not even another minute patch of pebbly beach. As the sun fell, so did our spirits. I had tried to make advances to the girl again; but she would have none of me, and so I was not only thirsty but otherwise sad and downhearted. I was glad when the new day broke the hideous spell of a sleepless night.

The morning's search brought us no shred of hope. Caprona was impregnable—that was the decision of all; yet we kept on. It must have been about two bells of the afternoon watch that Bradley called my attention to the branch of a tree, with leaves upon it, floating on the sea. "It may have been carried down to the ocean by a river," he suggested.

"Yes," I replied, "it may have; it may have tumbled or been thrown off the top of one of these cliffs."

Bradley's face fell. "I thought of that, too," he replied, "but I wanted to believe the other."

"Right you are!" I cried. "We must believe the other until we prove it false. We can't afford to give up heart now, when we need heart most. The branch was carried down by a river, and we are going to find that river." I smote my open palm with a clenched fist, to emphasize a determination unsupported by hope. "There!" I cried suddenly. "See that, Bradley?" And I pointed at a spot closer to shore. "See that, man!" Some flowers and grasses and another leafy branch floated toward us. We both scanned the water and the coastline. Bradley evidently discovered something, or at least thought that he had. He called down for a bucket and a rope, and when they were passed up to him, he lowered the former into the sea and drew it in filled with water. Of this he took a taste, and straightening up, looked into my eyes with an expression of elation—as much as to say "I told you so!"

"This water is warm," he announced, "and fresh!"

I grabbed the bucket and tasted its contents. The water was very warm, and it was fresh, but there was a most unpleasant taste to it.

"Did you ever taste water from a stagnant pool full of tadpoles?" Bradley asked.

"That's it," I exclaimed, "—that's just the taste exactly, though I haven't experienced it since boyhood; but how can water from a flowing stream, taste thus, and what the dickens makes it so warm? It must be at least 70 or 80 Fahrenheit, possibly higher."

"Yes," agreed Bradley, "I should say higher; but where does it come from?"

"That is easily discovered now that we have found it," I answered. "It can't come from the ocean; so it must come from the land. All that we have to do is follow it, and sooner or later we shall come upon its source."

We were already rather close in; but I ordered the *U-33*'s prow turned inshore and we crept slowly along, constantly dipping up the water and tasting it to assure ourselves that we didn't get outside the fresh-water current. There was a very light off-shore wind and scarcely any breakers, so that the approach to the shore was continued without finding bottom; yet though we were already quite close, we saw no indication of any indention in the coast from which even a tiny brooklet might issue, and certainly no mouth of a large river such as this must necessarily be to freshen the ocean even two hundred yards from shore. The tide was running out, and this, together with the strong flow of the freshwater current, would have prevented our going against the cliffs even had we not been under power; as it was we had to buck the combined forces in order to hold our position at all. We came up to within twenty-five feet of the sheer wall, which loomed high above us. There was no break in its forbidding face. As we watched the face of the waters and searched the cliff's high face, Olson suggested that the fresh water might come from a submarine geyser. This, he said, would account for its heat; but even as he spoke a bush, covered thickly with leaves and flowers, bubbled to the surface and floated off astern.

"Flowering shrubs don't thrive in the subterranean caverns from which geysers spring," suggested Bradley.

Olson shook his head. "It beats me," he said.

"I've got it!" I exclaimed suddenly. "Look there!" And I pointed at the base of the cliff ahead of us, which the receding tide was gradually exposing to our view. They all looked, and all saw what I had seen—the top of a dark opening in the rock, through which water was pouring out into the sea. "It's the subterranean channel of an inland river," I cried. "It flows through a land covered with vegetation—and therefore a land upon which the sun shines. No subterranean caverns produce any order of plant life even remotely resembling what we have seen disgorged by this river. Beyond those cliffs lie fertile lands and fresh water—perhaps, game!"

"Yis, sir," said Olson, "behoind the cliffs! Ye spoke a true word, sir—behoind!"

Bradley laughed—a rather sorry laugh, though. "You might as well call our attention to the fact, sir," he said, "that science has indicated that there is fresh water and vegetation on Mars."

"Not at all," I rejoined. "A U-boat isn't constructed to navigate space, but it is designed to travel below the surface of the water."

"You'd be after sailin' into that blank pocket?" asked Olson.

"I would, Olson," I replied. "We haven't one chance for life in a hundred thousand if we don't find food and water upon Caprona. This water coming out of the cliff is not salt; but neither is it fit to drink, though each of us has drunk. It is fair to assume that inland the river is fed by pure streams, that there are fruits and herbs and game. Shall we lie out here and die of thirst and starvation with a land of plenty possibly only a few hundred yards away? We have the means for navigating a subterranean river. Are we too cowardly to utilize this means?"

147

"Be afther goin' to it," said Olson.

"I'm willing to see it through," agreed Bradley.

"Then under the bottom, wi' the best o' luck an' give 'em hell!" cried a young fellow who had been in the trenches.

"To the diving-stations!" I commanded, and in less than a minute the deck was deserted, the conning-tower covers had slammed to and the *U-33* was submerging—possibly for the last time. I know that I had this feeling, and I think that most of the others did.

As we went down, I sat in the tower with the searchlight projecting its seemingly feeble rays ahead. We submerged very slowly and without headway more than sufficient to keep her nose in the right direction, and as we went down, I saw outlined ahead of us the black opening in the great cliff. It was an opening that would have admitted a half-dozen U-boats at one and the same time, roughly cylindrical in contour—and dark as the pit of perdition.

As I gave the command which sent the *U-33* slowly ahead, I could not but feel a certain uncanny presentiment of evil. Where were we going? What lay at the end of this great sewer? Had we bidden farewell forever to the sunlight and life, or were there before us dangers even greater than those which we now faced? I tried to keep my mind from vain imagining by calling everything which I observed to the eager ears below. I was the eyes of the whole company, and I did my best not to fail them. We had advanced a hundred yards, perhaps, when our first danger confronted us. Just ahead was a sharp right-angle turn in the tunnel. I could see the river's flotsam hurtling against the rocky wall upon the left as it was driven on by the mighty current, and I feared for the safety of the *U-33* in making so sharp a turn under such adverse conditions; but there was nothing for it but to try. I didn't warn my fellows of the danger—it could have but caused them useless apprehension, for if we were to be smashed against the rocky wall, no power on earth could avert the quick end that would come to us. I gave the command full speed ahead and went charging toward the menace. I was forced to approach the dangerous left-hand wall in order to make the turn, and I depended upon the power of the motors to carry us through the surging waters in safety. Well, we made it; but it was a narrow squeak. As we swung around, the full force of the current caught us and drove the stern against the rocks; there was a thud which sent a tremor through the whole craft, and then a moment of nasty grinding as the steel hull scraped the rock wall. I expected momentarily the inrush of waters that would seal our doom; but presently from below came the welcome word that all was well.

In another fifty yards there was a second turn, this time toward the left! but it was more of a gentle curve, and we took it without trouble. After that it was plain sailing, though as far as I could know, there might be most anything ahead of us, and my nerves strained to the snapping-point every instant. After the second turn the channel ran comparatively straight for between one hundred and fifty and two hundred yards. The waters grew suddenly lighter, and my spirits rose accordingly. I shouted down to those below that I saw daylight ahead, and a great shout of thanksgiving reverberated through the ship. A moment later we emerged into sunlit water, and immediately I raised the periscope and looked about me upon the strangest landscape I had ever seen.

We were in the middle of a broad and now sluggish river the banks of which were lined by giant, arboraceous ferns, raising their mighty fronds fifty, one hundred, two hundred feet into the quiet air. Close by us something rose to the surface of the river and dashed at the periscope. I had a vision of wide, distended jaws, and then all was blotted out. A shiver ran down into the tower as the thing closed upon the periscope. A moment later it was gone, and I could see again. Above the trees there soared into my vision a huge thing on batlike wings—a creature large as a large whale, but fashioned more after the order of a lizard. Then again something charged the periscope and blotted out the mirror. I will confess that I was almost gasping for breath as I gave the commands to emerge. Into what sort of strange land had fate guided us?

The instant the deck was awash, I opened the conning-tower hatch and stepped out. In another minute the deck-hatch lifted, and those who were not on duty below streamed up the ladder, Olson bringing Nobs under one arm. For several minutes no one spoke; I think they must each have been as overcome by awe as was I. All about us was a flora and fauna as strange and wonderful to us as might have been those upon a distant planet had we suddenly been miraculously transported through ether to an unknown world. Even the grass upon the nearer bank was unearthly—lush and high it grew, and each blade bore upon its tip a brilliant flower—violet or yellow or carmine or blue—making as gorgeous a sward as human imagination might conceive. But the life! It teemed. The tall, fernlike trees were alive with monkeys, snakes, and lizards. Huge insects hummed and buzzed hither and thither. Mighty forms could be seen moving upon the ground in the thick forest, while the bosom of the river wriggled with living things, and above flapped the wings of gigantic creatures such as we are taught have been extinct throughout countless ages.

"Look!" cried Olson. "Would you look at the giraffe comin' up out o' the bottom of the say?" We looked in the direction he pointed and saw a long, glossy neck surmounted by a small head rising above the surface of the river. Presently the back of the creature was exposed, brown and glossy as the water dripped from it. It turned its eyes upon us, opened its lizard-like mouth, emitted a shrill hiss and came for us. The thing must have been sixteen or eighteen feet in length and closely resembled pictures I had seen of restored plesiosaurs of the lower Jurassic. It charged us as savagely as a mad bull, and one would have thought it intended to destroy and devour the mighty U-boat, as I verily believe it did intend.

We were moving slowly up the river as the creature bore down upon us with distended jaws. The long neck was far outstretched, and the four flippers with which it swam were working with powerful strokes, carrying it forward at a rapid pace. When it reached the craft's side, the jaws closed upon one of the stanchions of the deck rail and tore it from its socket as though it had been a toothpick stuck in putty. At this exhibition of titanic strength I think we all simultaneously stepped backward, and Bradley drew his revolver and fired. The bullet struck the thing in the neck, just above its body; but instead of disabling it, merely increased its rage. Its hissing rose to a shrill scream as it raised half its body out of water onto the sloping sides of the hull of the *U-33* and endeavored to scramble upon the deck to devour us. A dozen shots rang out as we who were armed drew our pistols and fired at the thing; but though struck several times, it showed no signs of succumbing and only floundered farther aboard the submarine.

I had noticed that the girl had come on deck and was standing not far behind me, and when I saw the danger to which we were all exposed, I turned and forced her toward the hatch. We had not spoken for some days, and we did not speak now; but she gave me a disdainful look, which was quite as eloquent as words, and broke loose from my grasp. I saw I could do nothing with her unless I exerted force, and so I turned with my back toward her that I might be in a position to shield her from the strange reptile should it really succeed in reaching the deck; and as I did so I saw the thing raise one flipper over the rail, dart its head forward and with the quickness of lightning seize upon one of the boches. I ran forward, discharging my pistol into the creature's body in an effort to force it to relinquish its prey; but I might as profitably have shot at the sun.

Shrieking and screaming, the German was dragged from the deck, and the moment the reptile was clear of the boat, it dived beneath the surface of the water with its terrified prey. I think we were all more or less shaken by the frightfulness of the tragedy—until Olson remarked that the balance of power now rested where it belonged. Following the death of Benson we had been nine and nine—nine Germans and nine "Allies," as we called ourselves, now there were but eight Germans. We never counted the girl on either side, I suppose because she was a girl, though we knew well enough now that she was ours.

And so Olson's remark helped to clear the atmosphere for the Allies at least, and then our attention was once more directed toward the river, for around us there had sprung up a perfect bedlam of screams and hisses and a seething caldron of hideous reptiles, devoid of fear and filled only with hunger and with rage. They clambered, squirmed and wriggled to the deck, forcing us steadily backward, though we emptied our pistols into them. There were all sorts and conditions of horrible things—huge, hideous, grotesque, monstrous—a veritable Mesozoic nightmare. I saw that the girl was gotten below as quickly as possible, and she took Nobs with her— poor Nobs had nearly barked his head off; and I think, too, that for the first time since his littlest puppyhood he had known fear; nor can I blame him. After the girl I sent Bradley and most of the Allies and then the Germans who were on deck—von Schoenvorts being still in irons below.

The creatures were approaching perilously close before I dropped through the hatchway and slammed down the cover. Then I went into the tower and ordered full speed ahead, hoping to distance the fearsome things; but it was useless. Not only could any of them easily outdistance the *U-33*, but the further upstream we progressed the greater the number of our besiegers, until fearful of navigating a strange river at high speed, I gave orders to reduce and moved slowly and majestically through the plunging, hissing mass. I was mighty glad that our entrance into the interior of Caprona had been inside a submarine rather than in any other form of vessel. I could readily understand how it might have been that Caprona had been invaded in the past by venturesome navigators without word of it ever reaching the outside world, for I can assure you that only by submarine could man pass up that great sluggish river, alive.

We proceeded up the river for some forty miles before darkness overtook us. I was afraid to submerge and lie on the bottom overnight for fear that the mud might be deep enough to hold us, and as we could not hold with the anchor, I ran in close to shore, and in a brief interim of attack from the reptiles we made fast to a large tree. We also dipped up some of the river water and found it, though quite warm, a little sweeter than before. We had food enough, and with the water we were all quite refreshed; but we missed fresh meat. It had been weeks, now, since we had tasted it, and the sight of the reptiles gave me an idea—that a steak or two from one of them might not be bad eating. So I went on deck with a rifle, twenty of which were aboard the *U-33*. At sight of me a huge thing charged and climbed to the deck. I retreated to the top of the conning-tower, and when it had raised its mighty bulk to the level of the little deck on which I stood, I let it have a bullet right between the eyes.

The thing stopped then and looked at me a moment as much as to say: "Why this thing has a stinger! I must be careful." And then it reached out its long neck and opened its mighty jaws and grabbed for me; but I wasn't there. I had tumbled backward into the tower, and I mighty near killed myself doing it. When I glanced up, that little head on the end of its long neck was coming straight down on top of me, and once more I tumbled into greater safety, sprawling upon the floor of the centrale.

Olson was looking up, and seeing what was poking about in the tower, ran for an ax; nor did he hesitate a moment when he returned with one, but sprang up the ladder and commenced chopping away at that hideous face. The thing didn't have sufficient brainpan to entertain more than a single idea at once. Though chopped and hacked, and with a bullethole between its eyes, it still persisted madly in its attempt to get inside the tower and devour Olson, though its body was many times the diameter of the hatch; nor did it cease its efforts until after Olson had succeeded in decapitating it. Then the two men went on deck through the main hatch, and while one kept watch, the other cut a hind quarter off Plesiosaurus Olsoni, as Bradley dubbed the thing. Meantime Olson cut off the long neck, saying that it would make fine soup. By the time we had cleared away the blood and refuse in the tower, the cook had juicy steaks and a steaming broth upon the electric stove, and the aroma arising from P. Olsoni filled us all with a hitherto unfelt admiration for him and all his kind

CHAPTER FIVE

The steaks we had that night, and they were fine; and the following morning we tasted the broth. It seemed odd to be eating a creature that should, by all the laws of paleontology, have been extinct for several million years. It gave one a feeling of newness that was almost embarrassing, although it didn't seem to embarrass our appetites. Olson ate until I thought he would burst.

The girl ate with us that night at the little officers' mess just back of the torpedo compartment. The narrow table was unfolded; the four stools were set out; and for the first time in days we sat down to eat, and for the first time in weeks we had something to eat other than the monotony of the short rations of an impoverished U-boat. Nobs sat between the girl and me and was fed with morsels of the Plesiosaurus steak, at the risk of forever contaminating his manners. He looked at me sheepishly all the time, for he knew that no well-bred dog should eat at table; but the poor fellow was so wasted from improper food that I couldn't enjoy my own meal had he been denied an immediate share in it; and anyway Lys wanted to feed him. So there you are.

Lys was coldly polite to me and sweetly gracious to Bradley and Olson. She wasn't of the gushing type, I knew; so I didn't expect much from her and was duly grateful for the few morsels of attention she threw upon the floor to me. We had a pleasant meal, with only one unfortunate occurrence—when Olson suggested that possibly the creature we were eating was the same one that ate the German. It was some time before we could persuade the girl to continue her meal, but at last Bradley prevailed upon her, pointing out that we had come upstream nearly forty miles since the boche had been seized, and that during that time we had seen literally thousands of these denizens of the river, indicating that the chances were very remote that this was the same Plesiosaur. "And anyway," he concluded, "it was only a scheme of Mr. Olson's to get all the steaks for himself."

We discussed the future and ventured opinions as to what lay before us; but we could only theorize at best, for none of us knew. If the whole land was infested by these and similar horrid monsters, life would be impossible upon it, and we decided that we would only search long enough to find and take aboard fresh water and such meat and fruits as might be safely procurable and then retrace our way beneath the cliffs to the open sea.

And so at last we turned into our narrow bunks, hopeful, happy and at peace with ourselves, our lives and our God, to awaken the following morning refreshed and still optimistic. We had an easy time getting away—as we learned later, because the saurians do not commence to feed until late in the morning. From noon to midnight their curve of activity is at its height, while from dawn to about nine o'clock it is lowest. As a matter of fact, we didn't see one of them all the time we were getting under way, though I had the cannon raised to the deck and manned against an assault. I hoped, but I was none too sure, that shells might discourage them. The trees were full of monkeys of all sizes and shades, and once we thought we saw a manlike creature watching us from the depth of the forest.

Shortly after we resumed our course upstream, we saw the mouth of another and smaller river emptying into the main channel from the south—that is, upon our right; and almost immediately after we came upon a large island five or six miles in length; and at fifty miles there was a still larger river than the last coming in from the northwest, the course of the main stream having now changed to northeast by southwest. The water was quite free from reptiles, and the vegetation upon the banks of the river had altered to more open and parklike forest, with eucalyptus and acacia mingled with a scattering of tree ferns, as though two distinct periods of geologic time had overlapped and merged. The grass, too, was less flowering, though there were still gorgeous patches mottling the greensward; and lastly, the fauna was less multitudinous.

Six or seven miles farther, and the river widened considerably; before us opened an expanse of water to the farther horizon, and then we sailed out upon an inland sea so large that only a shore-line upon our side was visible to us. The waters all about us were alive with life. There were still a few reptiles; but there were fish by the thousands, by the millions.

The water of the inland sea was very warm, almost hot, and the atmosphere was hot and heavy above it. It seemed strange that beyond the buttressed walls of Caprona icebergs floated and the south wind was biting, for only a gentle breeze moved across the face of these living waters, and that was damp and warm. Gradually, we commenced to divest ourselves of our clothing, retaining only sufficient for modesty; but the sun was not hot. It was more the heat of a steam-room than of an oven.

We coasted up the shore of the lake in a north-westerly direction, sounding all the time. We found the lake deep and the bottom rocky and steeply shelving toward the center, and once when I moved straight out from shore to take other soundings we could find no bottom whatsoever. In open spaces along the shore we caught occasional glimpses of the distant cliffs, and here they appeared only a trifle less precipitous than those which bound Caprona on the seaward side. My theory is that in a far distant era Caprona was a mighty mountain—perhaps the world's mightiest mountain—and that in some titanic eruption volcanic action blew off the entire crest, blew thousands of feet of the mountain upward and outward and onto the surrounding continent, leaving a great crater; and then, possibly, the continent sank as ancient continents have been known to do, leaving only the summit of Caprona above the sea. The encircling walls, the central lake, the hot springs which feed the lake, all point to such a conclusion, and the fauna and the flora bear indisputable evidence that Caprona was once part of some great land-mass.

As we cruised up along the coast, the landscape continued a more or less open forest, with here and there a small plain where we saw animals grazing. With my glass I could make out a species of large red deer, some antelope and what appeared to be a species of horse; and once I saw the shaggy form of what might have been a monstrous bison. Here was game a plenty! There seemed little danger of starving upon Caprona. The game, however, seemed wary; for the instant the animals discovered us, they threw up their heads and tails and went cavorting off, those farther inland following the example of the others until all were lost in the mazes of the distant forest. Only the great, shaggy ox stood his ground. With lowered head he watched us until we had passed, and then continued feeding.

About twenty miles up the coast from the mouth of the river we encountered low cliffs of sandstone, broken and tortured evidence of the great upheaval which had torn Caprona asunder in the past, intermingling upon a common level the rock formations of widely separated eras, fusing some and leaving others untouched.

We ran along beside them for a matter of ten miles, arriving off a broad cleft which led into what appeared to be another lake. As we were in search of pure water, we did not wish to overlook any portion of the coast, and so after sounding and finding that we had ample depth, I ran the *U-33* between head-lands into as pretty a landlocked harbor as sailormen could care to see, with good water right up to within a few yards of the shore. As we cruised slowly along, two of the boches again saw what they believed to be a man, or manlike creature, watching us from a fringe of trees a hundred yards inland, and shortly after we discovered the mouth of a small stream emptying into the bay. It was the first stream we had found since leaving the river, and I at once made preparations to test its water. To land, it would be necessary to run the *U-33* close in to the shore, at least as close as we could, for even these waters were infested, though, not so thickly, by savage reptiles. I ordered sufficient water let into the diving-tanks to lower us about a foot, and then I ran the bow slowly toward the shore, confident that should we run aground, we still had sufficient lifting force to free us when the water should be pumped out of the tanks; but the bow nosed its way gently into the reeds and touched the shore with the keel still clear.

My men were all armed now with both rifles and pistols, each having plenty of ammunition. I ordered one of the Germans ashore with a line, and sent two of my own men to guard him, for from what little we had seen of Caprona, or Caspak as we learned later to call the interior, we realized that any instant some new and terrible danger might confront us. The line was made fast to a small tree, and at the same time I had the stern anchor dropped.

As soon as the boche and his guard were aboard again, I called all hands on deck, including von Schoenvorts, and there I explained to them that the time had come for us to enter into some sort of an agreement among ourselves that would relieve us of the annoyance and embarrassment of being divided into two antagonistic parts—prisoners and captors. I told them that it was obvious our very existence depended upon our unity of action, that we were to all intent and purpose entering a new world as far from the seat and causes of our own world-war as if millions of miles of space and eons of time separated us from our past lives and habitations.

"There is no reason why we should carry our racial and political hatreds into Caprona," I insisted. "The Germans among us might kill all the English, or the English might kill the last German, without affecting in the slightest degree either the outcome of even the smallest skirmish upon the western front or the opinion of a single individual in any belligerent or neutral country. I therefore put the issue squarely to you all; shall we bury our animosities and work together with and for one another while we remain upon Caprona, or must we continue thus divided and but half armed, possibly until death has claimed the last of us? And let me tell you, if you have not already realized it, the chances are a thousand to one that not one of us ever will see the outside world again. We are safe now in the matter of food and water; we could provision the *U-33* for a long cruise; but we are practically out of fuel, and without fuel we cannot hope to reach the ocean, as only a submarine can pass through the barrier cliffs. What is your answer?" I turned toward von Schoenvorts.

He eyed me in that disagreeable way of his and demanded to know, in case they accepted my suggestion, what their status would be in event of our finding a way to escape with the *U-33*. I replied that I felt that if we had all worked loyally together we should leave Caprona upon a common footing, and to that end I suggested that should the remote possibility of our escape in the submarine develop into reality, we should then immediately make for the nearest neutral port and give ourselves into the hands of the authorities, when we should all probably be interned for the duration of the war. To my surprise he agreed that this was fair and told me that they would accept my conditions and that I could depend upon their loyalty to the common cause.

I thanked him and then addressed each one of his men individually, and each gave me his word that he would abide by all that I had outlined. It was further understood that we were to act as a military organization under military rules and discipline—I as commander, with Bradley as my first lieutenant and Olson as my second, in command of the Englishmen; while von Schoenvorts was to act as an additional second lieutenant and have charge of his own men. The four of us were to constitute a military court under which men might be tried and sentenced to punishment for infraction of military rules and discipline, even to the passing of the death-sentence.

I then had arms and ammunition issued to the Germans, and leaving Bradley and five men to guard the *U-33*, the balance of us went ashore. The first thing we did was to taste the water of the little stream—which, to our delight, we found sweet, pure and cold. This stream was entirely free from dangerous reptiles, because, as I later discovered, they became immediately dormant when subjected to a much lower temperature than 70 degrees Fahrenheit. They dislike cold water and keep as far away from it as possible. There were countless brook-trout here, and deep holes that invited us to bathe, and along the bank of the stream were trees bearing a close resemblance to ash and beech and oak, their characteristics evidently induced by the lower temperature of the air above the cold water and by the fact that their roots were watered by the water from the stream rather than from the warm springs which we afterward found in such abundance elsewhere.

Our first concern was to fill the water tanks of the *U-33* with fresh water, and that having been accomplished, we set out to hunt for game and explore inland for a short distance. Olson, von Schoenvorts, two Englishmen and two Germans accompanied me, leaving ten to guard the ship and the girl. I had intended leaving Nobs behind, but he got away and joined me and was so happy over it that I hadn't the heart to send him back. We followed the stream upward through a beautiful country for about five miles, and then came upon its source in a little boulder-strewn clearing. From among the rocks bubbled fully twenty ice-cold springs. North of the clearing rose sandstone cliffs to a height of some fifty to seventy-five feet, with tall trees growing at their base and almost concealing them from our view. To the west the country was flat and sparsely wooded, and here it was that we saw our first game—a large red deer. It was grazing away from us and had not seen us when one of my men called my attention to it. Motioning for silence and having the rest of the party lie down, I crept toward the quarry, accompanied only by Whitely. We got within a hundred yards of the deer when he suddenly raised his antlered head and pricked up his great ears. We both fired at once and had the satisfaction of seeing the buck drop; then we ran forward to finish him with our knives. The deer lay in a small open space close to a clump of acacias, and we had advanced to within several yards of our kill when we both halted suddenly and simultaneously. Whitely looked at me, and I looked at Whitely, and then we both looked back in the direction of the deer.

"Blime!" he said. "Wot is hit, sir?"

"It looks to me, Whitely, like an error," I said; "some assistant god who had been creating elephants must have been temporarily transferred to the lizard-department."

"Hi wouldn't s'y that, sir," said Whitely; "it sounds blasphemous."

"It is no more blasphemous than that thing which is swiping our meat," I replied, for whatever the thing was, it had leaped upon our deer and was devouring it in great mouthfuls which it swallowed without mastication. The creature appeared to be a great lizard at least ten feet high, with a huge, powerful tail as long as its torso, mighty hind legs and short forelegs. When it had advanced from the wood, it hopped much after the fashion of a kangaroo, using its hind feet and tail to propel it, and when it stood erect, it sat upon its tail. Its head was long and thick, with a blunt muzzle, and the opening of the jaws ran back to a point behind the eyes, and the jaws were armed with long sharp teeth. The scaly body was covered with black and yellow spots about a foot in diameter and irregular in contour. These spots were outlined in red with edgings about an inch wide. The underside of the chest, body and tail were a greenish white.

"Wot s'y we pot the bloomin' bird, sir?" suggested Whitely.

I told him to wait until I gave the word; then we would fire simultaneously, he at the heart and I at the spine.

"Hat the 'eart, sir—yes, sir," he replied, and raised his piece to his shoulder.

Our shots rang out together. The thing raised its head and looked about until its eyes rested upon us; then it gave vent to a most appalling hiss that rose to the crescendo of a terrific shriek and came for us.

"Beat it, Whitely!" I cried as I turned to run.

We were about a quarter of a mile from the rest of our party, and in full sight of them as they lay in the tall grass watching us. That they saw all that had happened was evidenced by the fact that they now rose and ran toward us, and at their head leaped Nobs. The creature in our rear was gaining on us rapidly when Nobs flew past me like a meteor and rushed straight for the frightful reptile. I tried to recall him, but he would pay no attention to me, and as I couldn't see him sacrificed, I, too, stopped and faced the monster. The creature appeared to be more impressed with Nobs than by us and our firearms, for it stopped as the Airedale dashed at it growling, and struck at him viciously with its powerful jaws.

Nobs, though, was lightning by comparison with the slow thinking beast and dodged his opponent's thrust with ease. Then he raced to the rear of the tremendous thing and seized it by the tail. There Nobs made the error of his life. Within that mottled organ were the muscles of a Titan, the force of a dozen mighty catapults, and the owner of the tail was fully aware of the possibilities which it contained. With a single flip of the tip it sent poor Nobs sailing through the air a hundred feet above the ground, straight back into the clump of acacias from which the beast had leaped upon our kill— and then the grotesque thing sank lifeless to the ground.

Olson and von Schoenvorts came up a minute later with their men; then we all cautiously approached the still form upon the ground. The creature was quite dead, and an examination resulted in disclosing the fact that Whitely's bullet had pierced its heart, and mine had severed the spinal cord.

"But why didn't it die instantly?" I exclaimed.

"Because," said von Schoenvorts in his disagreeable way, "the beast is so large, and its nervous organization of so low a caliber, that it took all this time for the intelligence of death to reach and be impressed upon the minute brain. The thing was dead when your bullets struck it; but it did not know it for several seconds—possibly a minute. If I am not mistaken, it is an Allosaurus of the Upper Jurassic, remains of which have been found in Central Wyoming, in the suburbs of New York."

An Irishman by the name of Brady grinned. I afterward learned that he had served three years on the traffic-squad of the Chicago police force.

I had been calling Nobs in the meantime and was about to set out in search of him, fearing, to tell the truth, to do so lest I find him mangled and dead among the trees of the acacia grove, when he suddenly emerged from among the boles, his ears flattened, his tail between his legs and his body screwed into a suppliant S. He was unharmed except for minor bruises; but he was the most chastened dog I have ever seen.

We gathered up what was left of the red deer after skinning and cleaning it, and set out upon our return journey toward the U-boat. On the way Olson, von Schoenvorts and I discussed the needs of our immediate future, and we were unanimous in placing foremost the necessity of a permanent camp on shore. The interior of a U-boat is about as impossible and uncomfortable an abiding-place as one can well imagine, and in this warm climate, and in warm water, it was almost unendurable. So we decided to construct a palisaded camp

CHAPTER SIX

As we strolled slowly back toward the boat, planning and discussing this, we were suddenly startled by a loud and unmistakable detonation.

"A shell from the *U-33*!" exclaimed von Schoenvorts.

"What can be after signifyin'?" queried Olson.

"They are in trouble," I answered for all, "and it's up to us to get back to them. Drop that carcass," I directed the men carrying the meat, "and follow me!" I set off at a rapid run in the direction of the harbor.

We ran for the better part of a mile without hearing anything more from the direction of the harbor, and then I reduced the speed to a walk, for the exercise was telling on us who had been cooped up for so long in the confined interior of the *U-33*. Puffing and panting, we plodded on until within about a mile of the harbor we came upon a sight that brought us all up standing. We had been passing through a little heavier timber than was usual to this part of the country, when we suddenly emerged into an open space in the center of which was such a band as might have caused the most courageous to pause. It consisted of upward of five hundred individuals representing several species closely allied to man. There were anthropoid apes and gorillas—these I had no difficulty in recognizing; but there were other forms which I had never before seen, and I was hard put to it to say whether they were ape or man. Some of them resembled the corpse we had found upon the narrow beach against Caprona's sea-wall, while others were of a still lower type, more nearly resembling the apes, and yet others were uncannily manlike, standing there erect, being less hairy and possessing better shaped heads.

There was one among the lot, evidently the leader of them, who bore a close resemblance to the so-called Neanderthal man of La Chapelle-aux-Saints. There was the same short, stocky trunk upon which rested an enormous head habitually bent forward into the same curvature as the back, the arms shorter than the legs, and the lower leg considerably shorter than that of modern man, the knees bent forward and never straightened. This creature and one or two others who appeared to be of a lower order than he, yet higher than that of the apes, carried heavy clubs; the others were armed only with giant muscles and fighting fangs— nature's weapons. All were males, and all were entirely naked; nor was there upon even the highest among them a sign of ornamentation.

At sight of us they turned with bared fangs and low growls to confront us. I did not wish to fire among them unless it became absolutely necessary, and so I started to lead my party around them; but the instant that the Neanderthal man guessed my intention, he evidently attributed it to cowardice upon our part, and with a wild cry he leaped toward us, waving his cudgel above his head. The others followed him, and in a minute we should have been overwhelmed. I gave the order to fire, and at the first volley six of them went down, including the Neanderthal man. The others hesitated a moment and then broke for the trees, some running nimbly among the branches, while others lost themselves to us between the boles. Both von Schoenvorts and I noticed that at least two of the higher, manlike types took to the trees quite as nimbly as the apes, while others that more nearly approached man in carriage and appearance sought safety upon the ground with the gorillas.

An examination disclosed that five of our erstwhile opponents were dead and the sixth, the Neanderthal man, was but slightly wounded, a bullet having glanced from his thick skull, stunning him. We decided to take him with us to camp, and by means of belts we managed to secure his hands behind his back and place a leash around his neck before he regained consciousness. We then retraced our steps for our meat being convinced by our own experience that those aboard the U-33 had been able to frighten off this party with a single shell—but when we came to where we had left the deer it had disappeared.

On the return journey Whitely and I preceded the rest of the party by about a hundred yards in the hope of getting another shot at something edible, for we were all greatly disgusted and disappointed by the loss of our venison. Whitely and I advanced very cautiously, and not having the whole party with us, we fared better than on the journey out, bagging two large antelope not a half-mile from the harbor; so with our game and our prisoner we made a cheerful return to the boat, where we found that all were safe. On the shore a little north of where we lay there were the corpses of twenty of the wild creatures who had attacked Bradley and his party in our absence, and the rest of whom we had met and scattered a few minutes later.

We felt that we had taught these wild ape-men a lesson and that because of it we would be safer in the future—at least safer from them; but we decided not to abate our carefulness one whit, feeling that this new world was filled with terrors still unknown to us; nor were we wrong.

The following morning we commenced work upon our camp, Bradley, Olson, von Schoenvorts, Miss La Rue, and I having sat up half the night discussing the matter and drawing plans. We set the men at work felling trees, selecting for the purpose jarrah, a hard, weather-resisting timber which grew in profusion near by. Half the men labored while the other half stood guard, alternating each hour with an hour off at noon. Olson directed this work. Bradley, von Schoenvorts and I, with Miss La Rue's help, staked out the various buildings and the outer wall. When the day was done, we had quite an array of logs nicely notched and ready for our building operations on the morrow, and we were all tired, for after the buildings had been staked out we all fell in and helped with the logging—all but von Schoenvorts. He, being a Prussian and a gentleman, couldn't stoop to such menial labor in the presence of his men, and I didn't see fit to ask it of him, as the work was purely voluntary upon our part. He spent the afternoon shaping a swagger-stick from the branch of jarrah and talking with Miss La Rue, who had sufficiently unbent toward him to notice his existence.

We saw nothing of the wild men of the previous day, and only once were we menaced by any of the strange denizens of Caprona, when some frightful nightmare of the sky swooped down upon us, only to be driven off by a fusillade of bullets. The thing appeared to be some variety of pterodactyl, and what with its enormous size and ferocious aspect was most awe-inspiring. There was another incident, too, which to me at least was far more unpleasant than the sudden onslaught of the prehistoric reptile. Two of the men, both Germans, were stripping a felled tree of its branches. Von Schoenvorts had completed his swagger-stick, and he and I were passing close to where the two worked.

One of them threw to his rear a small branch that he had just chopped off, and as misfortune would have it, it struck von Schoenvorts across the face. It couldn't have hurt him, for it didn't leave a mark; but he flew into a terrific rage, shouting: "Attention!" in a loud voice. The sailor immediately straightened up, faced his officer, clicked his heels together and saluted. "Pig!" roared the Baron, and struck the fellow across the face, breaking his nose. I grabbed von Schoenvorts' arm and jerked him away before he could strike again, if such had been his intention, and then he raised his little stick to strike me; but before it descended the muzzle of my pistol was against his belly and he must have seen in my eyes that nothing would suit me better than an excuse to pull the trigger. Like all his kind and all other bullies, von Schoenvorts was a coward at heart, and so he dropped his hand to his side and started to turn away; but I pulled him back, and there before his men I told him that such a thing must never again occur—that no man was to be struck or otherwise punished other than in due process of the laws that we had made and the court that we had established. All the time the sailor stood rigidly at attention, nor could I tell from his expression whether he most resented the blow his officer had struck him or my interference in the gospel of the Kaiser-breed. Nor did he move until I said to him: "Plesser, you may return to your quarters and dress your wound." Then he saluted and marched stiffly off toward the *U-33*.

Just before dusk we moved out into the bay a hundred yards from shore and dropped anchor, for I felt that we should be safer there than elsewhere. I also detailed men to stand watch during the night and appointed Olson officer of the watch for the entire night, telling him to bring his blankets on deck and get what rest he could. At dinner we tasted our first roast Caprona antelope, and we had a mess of greens that the cook had found growing along the stream. All during the meal von Schoenvorts was silent and surly.

After dinner we all went on deck and watched the unfamiliar scenes of a Capronian night—that is, all but von Schoenvorts. There was less to see than to hear. From the great inland lake behind us came the hissing and the screaming of countless saurians. Above us we heard the flap of giant wings, while from the shore rose the multitudinous voices of a tropical jungle—of a warm, damp atmosphere such as must have enveloped the entire earth during the Palezeoic and Mesozoic eras. But here were intermingled the voices of later eras—the scream of the panther, the roar of the lion, the baying of wolves and a thunderous growling which we could attribute to nothing earthly but which one day we were to connect with the most fearsome of ancient creatures.

One by one the others went to their rooms, until the girl and I were left alone together, for I had permitted the watch to go below for a few minutes, knowing that I would be on deck. Miss La Rue was very quiet, though she replied graciously enough to whatever I had to say that required reply. I asked her if she did not feel well.

"Yes," she said, "but I am depressed by the awfulness of it all. I feel of so little consequence—so small and helpless in the face of all these myriad manifestations of life stripped to the bone of its savagery and brutality. I realize as never before how cheap and valueless a thing is life. Life seems a joke, a cruel, grim joke. You are a laughable incident or a terrifying one as you happen to be less powerful or more powerful than some other form of life which crosses your path; but as a rule you are of no moment whatsoever to anything but yourself. You are a comic little figure, hopping from the cradle to the grave. Yes, that is our trouble—we take ourselves too seriously; but Caprona should be a sure cure for that." She paused and laughed.

"You have evolved a beautiful philosophy," I said. "It fills such a longing in the human breast. It is full, it is satisfying, it is ennobling. What wondrous strides toward perfection the human race might have made if the first man had evolved it and it had persisted until now as the creed of humanity."

"I don't like irony," she said; "it indicates a small soul."

"What other sort of soul, then, would you expect from `a comic little figure hopping from the cradle to the grave'?" I inquired. "And what difference does it make, anyway, what you like and what you don't like? You are here for but an instant, and you mustn't take yourself too seriously."

She looked up at me with a smile. "I imagine that I am frightened and blue," she said, "and I know that I am very, very homesick and lonely." There was almost a sob in her voice as she concluded. It was the first time that she had spoken thus to me. Involuntarily, I laid my hand upon hers where it rested on the rail.

"I know how difficult your position is," I said; "but don't feel that you are alone. There is—is one here who—who would do anything in the world for you," I ended lamely. She did not withdraw her hand, and she looked up into my face with tears on her cheeks and I read in her eyes the thanks her lips could not voice. Then she looked away across the weird moonlit landscape and sighed. Evidently her new-found philosophy had tumbled about her ears, for she was seemingly taking herself seriously. I wanted to take her in my arms and tell her how I loved her, and had taken her hand from the rail and started to draw her toward me when Olson came blundering up on deck with his bedding.

The following morning we started building operations in earnest, and things progressed finely. The Neanderthal man was something of a care, for we had to keep him in irons all the time, and he was mighty savage when approached; but after a time he became more docile, and then we tried to discover if he had a language. Lys spent a great deal of time talking to him and trying to draw him out; but for a long while she was unsuccessful. It took us three weeks to build all the houses, which we constructed close by a cold spring some two miles from the harbor.

We changed our plans a trifle when it came to building the palisade, for we found a rotted cliff near by where we could get all the flat building-stone we needed, and so we constructed a stone wall entirely around the buildings. It was in the form of a square, with bastions and towers at each corner which would permit an enfilading fire along any side of the fort, and was about one hundred and thirty-five feet square on the outside, with walls three feet thick at the bottom and about a foot and a half wide at the top, and fifteen feet high. It took a long time to build that wall, and we all turned in and helped except von Schoenvorts, who, by the way, had not spoken to me except in the line of official business since our encounter—a condition of armed neutrality which suited me to a T. We have just finished it, the last touches being put on today. I quit about a week ago and commenced working on this chronicle for our strange adventures, which will account for any minor errors in chronology which may have crept in; there was so much material that I may have made some mistakes, but I think they are but minor and few.

I see in reading over the last few pages that I neglected to state that Lys finally discovered that the Neanderthal man possessed a language. She has learned to speak it, and so have I, to some extent. It was he—his name he says is Am, or Ahm—who told us that this country is called Caspak. When we asked him how far it extended, he waved both arms about his head in an all-including gesture which took in, apparently, the entire universe. He is more tractable now, and we are going to release him, for he has assured us that he will not permit his fellows to harm us. He calls us Galus and says that in a short time he will be a Galu. It is not quite clear to us what he means. He says that there are many Galus north of us, and that as soon as he becomes one he will go and live with them.

Ahm went out to hunt with us yesterday and was much impressed by the ease with which our rifles brought down antelopes and deer. We have been living upon the fat of the land, Ahm having shown us the edible fruits, tubers and herbs, and twice a week we go out after fresh meat. A certain proportion of this we dry and store away, for we do not know what may come. Our drying process is really smoking. We have also dried a large quantity of two varieties of cereal which grow wild a few miles south of us. One of these is a giant Indian maize—a lofty perennial often fifty and sixty feet in height, with ears the size of a man's body and kernels as large as your fist. We have had to construct a second store house for the great quantity of this that we have gathered.

September 3, 1916: Three months ago today the torpedo from the *U-33* started me from the peaceful deck of the American liner upon the strange voyage which has ended here in Caspak. We have settled down to an acceptance of our fate, for all are convinced that none of us will ever see the outer world again. Ahm's repeated assertions that there are human beings like ourselves in Caspak have roused the men to a keen desire for exploration. I sent out one party last week under Bradley. Ahm, who is now free to go and come as he wishes, accompanied them. They marched about twenty-five miles due west, encountering many terrible beasts and reptiles and not a few manlike creatures whom Ahm sent away. Here is Bradley's report of the expedition:

Marched fifteen miles the first day, camping on the bank of a large stream which runs southward. Game was plentiful and we saw several varieties which we had not before encountered in Caspak. Just before making camp we were charged by an enormous woolly rhinoceros, which Plesser dropped with a perfect shot. We had rhinoceros-steaks for supper. Ahm called the thing "Atis." It was almost a continuous battle from the time we left the fort until we arrived at camp. The mind of man can scarce conceive the plethora of carnivorous life in this lost world; and their prey, of course, is even more abundant.

The second day we marched about ten miles to the foot of the cliffs. Passed through dense forests close to the base of the cliffs. Saw manlike creatures and a low order of ape in one band, and some of the men swore that there was a white man among them. They were inclined to attack us at first; but a volley from our rifles caused them to change their minds. We scaled the cliffs as far as we could; but near the top they are absolutely perpendicular without any sufficient cleft or protuberance to give hand or foot-hold. All were disappointed, for we hungered for a view of the ocean and the outside world. We even had a hope that we might see and attract the attention of a passing ship. Our exploration has determined one thing which will probably be of little value to us and never heard of beyond Caprona's walls—this crater was once entirely filled with water. Indisputable evidence of this is on the face of the cliffs.

Our return journey occupied two days and was as filled with adventure as usual. We are all becoming accustomed to adventure. It is beginning to pall on us. We suffered no casualties and there was no illness.

I had to smile as I read Bradley's report. In those four days he had doubtless passed through more adventures than an African big-game hunter experiences in a lifetime, and yet he covered it all in a few lines. Yes, we are becoming accustomed to adventure. Not a day passes that one or more of us does not face death at least once. Ahm taught us a few things that have proved profitable and saved us much ammunition, which it is useless to expend except for food or in the last recourse of self-preservation. Now when we are attacked by large flying reptiles we run beneath spreading trees; when land carnivora threaten us, we climb into trees, and we have learned not to fire at any of the dinosaurs unless we can keep out of their reach for at least two minutes after hitting them in the brain or spine, or five minutes after puncturing their hearts—it takes them so long to die. To hit them elsewhere is worse than useless, for they do not seem to notice it, and we had discovered that such shots do not kill or even disable them.

September 7, 1916: Much has happened since I last wrote. Bradley is away again on another exploration expedition to the cliffs. He expects to be gone several weeks and to follow along their base in search of a point where they may be scaled. He took Sinclair, Brady, James, and Tippet with him. Ahm has disappeared. He has been gone about three days; but the most startling thing I have on record is that von Schoenvorts and Olson while out hunting the other day discovered oil about fifteen miles north of us beyond the sandstone cliffs. Olson says there is a geyser of oil there, and von Schoenvorts is making preparations to refine it. If he succeeds, we shall have the means for leaving Caspak and returning to our own world. I can scarce believe the truth of it. We are all elated to the seventh heaven of bliss. Pray God we shall not be disappointed.

I have tried on several occasions to broach the subject of my love to Lys; but she will not listen.

CHAPTER SEVEN

October 8, 1916: This is the last entry I shall make upon my manuscript. When this is done, I shall be through. Though I may pray that it reaches the haunts of civilized man, my better judgment tells me that it will never be perused by other eyes than mine, and that even though it should, it would be too late to avail me. I am alone upon the summit of the great cliff overlooking the broad Pacific. A chill south wind bites at my marrow, while far below me I can see the tropic foliage of Caspak on the one hand and huge icebergs from the near Antarctic upon the other. Presently I shall stuff my folded manuscript into the thermos bottle I have carried with me for the purpose since I left the fort—Fort Dinosaur we named it—and hurl it far outward over the cliff-top into the Pacific. What current washes the shore of Caprona I know not; whither my bottle will be borne I cannot even guess; but I have done all that mortal man may do to notify the world of my whereabouts and the dangers that threaten those of us who remain alive in Caspak—if there be any other than myself.

About the 8th of September I accompanied Olson and von Schoenvorts to the oil-geyser. Lys came with us, and we took a number of things which von Schoenvorts wanted for the purpose of erecting a crude refinery. We went up the coast some ten or twelve miles in the *U-33*, tying up to shore near the mouth of a small stream which emptied great volumes of crude oil into the sea—I find it difficult to call this great lake by any other name. Then we disembarked and went inland about five miles, where we came upon a small lake entirely filled with oil, from the center of which a geyser of oil spouted.

On the edge of the lake we helped von Schoenvorts build his primitive refinery. We worked with him for two days until he got things fairly well started, and then we returned to Fort Dinosaur, as I feared that Bradley might return and be worried by our absence. The *U-33* merely landed those of us that were to return to the fort and then retraced its course toward the oil-well. Olson, Whitely, Wilson, Miss La Rue, and myself disembarked, while von Schoenvorts and his German crew returned to refine the oil. The next day Plesser and two other Germans came down overland for ammunition. Plesser said they had been attacked by wild men and had exhausted a great deal of ammunition. He also asked permission to get some dried meat and maize, saying that they were so busy with the work of refining that they had no time to hunt. I let him have everything he asked for, and never once did a suspicion of their intentions enter my mind. They returned to the oil-well the same day, while we continued with the multitudinous duties of camp life.

For three days nothing of moment occurred. Bradley did not return; nor did we have any word from von Schoenvorts. In the evening Lys and I went up into one of the bastion towers and listened to the grim and terrible nightlife of the frightful ages of the past. Once a saber-tooth screamed almost beneath us, and the girl shrank close against me. As I felt her body against mine, all the pent love of these three long months shattered the bonds of timidity and conviction, and I swept her up into my arms and covered her face and lips with kisses. She did not struggle to free herself; but instead her dear arms crept up about my neck and drew my own face even closer to hers.

"You love me, Lys?" I cried.

I felt her head nod an affirmative against my breast. "Tell me, Lys," I begged, "tell me in words how much you love me."

Low and sweet and tender came the answer: "I love you beyond all conception."

My heart filled with rapture then, and it fills now as it has each of the countless times I have recalled those dear words, as it shall fill always until death has claimed me. I may never see her again; she may not know how I love her—she may question, she may doubt; but always true and steady, and warm with the fires of love my heart beats for the girl who said that night: "I love you beyond all conception."

For a long time we sat there upon the little bench constructed for the sentry that we had not as yet thought it necessary to post in more than one of the four towers. We learned to know one another better in those two brief hours than we had in all the months that had intervened since we had been thrown together. She told me that she had loved me from the first, and that she never had loved von Schoenvorts, their engagement having been arranged by her aunt for social reasons.

That was the happiest evening of my life; nor ever do I expect to experience its like; but at last, as is the way of happiness, it terminated. We descended to the compound, and I walked with Lys to the door of her quarters. There again she kissed me and bade me good night, and then she went in and closed the door.

I went to my own room, and there I sat by the light of one of the crude candles we had made from the tallow of the beasts we had killed, and lived over the events of the evening. At last I turned in and fell asleep, dreaming happy dreams and planning for the future, for even in savage Caspak I was bound to make my girl safe and happy. It was daylight when I awoke. Wilson, who was acting as cook, was up and astir at his duties in the cook-house. The others slept; but I arose and followed by Nobs went down to the stream for a plunge. As was our custom, I went armed with both rifle and revolver; but I stripped and had my swim without further disturbance than the approach of a large hyena, a number of which occupied caves in the sand-stone cliffs north of the camp. These brutes are enormous and exceedingly ferocious. I imagine they correspond with the cave-hyena of prehistoric times. This fellow charged Nobs, whose Capronian experiences had taught him that discretion is the better part of valor—with the result that he dived head foremost into the stream beside me after giving vent to a series of ferocious growls which had no more effect upon Hyaena spelaeus than might a sweet smile upon an enraged tusker. Afterward I shot the beast, and Nobs had a feast while I dressed, for he had become quite a raw-meat eater during our numerous hunting expeditions, upon which we always gave him a portion of the kill.

Whitely and Olson were up and dressed when we returned, and we all sat down to a good breakfast. I could not but wonder at Lys' absence from the table, for she had always been one of the earliest risers in camp; so about nine o'clock, becoming apprehensive lest she might be indisposed, I went to the door of her room and knocked. I received no response, though I finally pounded with all my strength; then I turned the knob and entered, only to find that she was not there. Her bed had been occupied, and her clothing lay where she had placed it the previous night upon retiring; but Lys was gone. To say that I was distracted with terror would be to put it mildly. Though I knew she could not be in camp, I searched every square inch of the compound and all the buildings, yet without avail.

It was Whitely who discovered the first clue—a huge human-like footprint in the soft earth beside the spring, and indications of a struggle in the mud.

Then I found a tiny handkerchief close to the outer wall. Lys had been stolen! It was all too plain. Some hideous member of the ape-man tribe had entered the fort and carried her off. While I stood stunned and horrified at the frightful evidence before me, there came from the direction of the great lake an increasing sound that rose to the volume of a shriek. We all looked up as the noise approached apparently just above us, and a moment later there followed a terrific explosion which hurled us to the ground. When we clambered to our feet, we saw a large section of the west wall torn and shattered. It was Olson who first recovered from his daze sufficiently to guess the explanation of the phenomenon.

"A shell!" he cried. "And there ain't no shells in Caspak besides what's on the *U-33*. The dirty boches are shellin' the fort. Come on!" And he grasped his rifle and started on a run toward the lake. It was over two miles, but we did not pause until the harbor was in view, and still we could not see the lake because of the sandstone cliffs which intervened. We ran as fast as we could around the lower end of the harbor, scrambled up the cliffs and at last stood upon their summit in full view of the lake. Far away down the coast, toward the river through which we had come to reach the lake, we saw upon the surface the outline of the *U-33*, black smoke vomiting from her funnel.

Von Schoenvorts had succeeded in refining the oil! The cur had broken his every pledge and was leaving us there to our fates. He had even shelled the fort as a parting compliment; nor could anything have been more truly Prussian than this leave-taking of the Baron Friedrich von Schoenvorts.

Olson, Whitely, Wilson, and I stood for a moment looking at one another. It seemed incredible that man could be so perfidious—that we had really seen with our own eyes the thing that we had seen; but when we returned to the fort, the shattered wall gave us ample evidence that there was no mistake.

Then we began to speculate as to whether it had been an ape-man or a Prussian that had abducted Lys. From what we knew of von Schoenvorts, we would not have been surprised at anything from him; but the footprints by the spring seemed indisputable evidence that one of Caprona's undeveloped men had borne off the girl I loved.

As soon as I had assured myself that such was the case, I made my preparations to follow and rescue her. Olson, Whitely, and Wilson each wished to accompany me; but I told them that they were needed here, since with Bradley's party still absent and the Germans gone it was necessary that we conserve our force as far as might be possible.

CHAPTER EIGHT

It was a sad leave-taking as in silence I shook hands with each of the three remaining men. Even poor Nobs appeared dejected as we quit the compound and set out upon the well-marked spoor of the abductor. Not once did I turn my eyes backward toward Fort Dinosaur. I have not looked upon it since—nor in all likelihood shall I ever look upon it again. The trail led northwest until it reached the western end of the sandstone cliffs to the north of the fort; there it ran into a well-defined path which wound northward into a country we had not as yet explored. It was a beautiful, gently rolling country, broken by occasional outcroppings of sandstone and by patches of dense forest relieved by open, park-like stretches and broad meadows whereon grazed countless herbivorous animals—red deer, aurochs, and infinite variety of antelope and at least three distinct species of horse, the latter ranging in size from a creature about as large as Nobs to a magnificent animal fourteen to sixteen hands high. These creatures fed together in perfect amity; nor did they show any great indications of terror when Nobs and I approached. They moved out of our way and kept their eyes upon us until we had passed; then they resumed their feeding.

The path led straight across the clearing into another forest, lying upon the verge of which I saw a bit of white. It appeared to stand out in marked contrast and incongruity to all its surroundings, and when I stopped to examine it, I found that it was a small strip of muslin—part of the hem of a garment. At once I was all excitement, for I knew that it was a sign left by Lys that she had been carried this way; it was a tiny bit torn from the hem of the undergarment that she wore in lieu of the night-robes she had lost with the sinking of the liner. Crushing the bit of fabric to my lips, I pressed on even more rapidly than before, because I now knew that I was upon the right trail and that up to this point at least, Lys still had lived.

I made over twenty miles that day, for I was now hardened to fatigue and accustomed to long hikes, having spent considerable time hunting and exploring in the immediate vicinity of camp. A dozen times that day was my life threatened by fearsome creatures of the earth or sky, though I could not but note that the farther north I traveled, the fewer were the great dinosaurs, though they still persisted in lesser numbers. On the other hand the quantity of ruminants and the variety and frequency of carnivorous animals increased. Each square mile of Caspak harbored its terrors.

At intervals along the way I found bits of muslin, and often they reassured me when otherwise I should have been doubtful of the trail to take where two crossed or where there were forks, as occurred at several points. And so, as night was drawing on, I came to the southern end of a line of cliffs loftier than any I had seen before, and as I approached them, there was wafted to my nostrils the pungent aroma of woodsmoke. What could it mean? There could, to my mind, be but a single solution: man abided close by, a higher order of man than we had as yet seen, other than Ahm, the Neanderthal man. I wondered again as I had so many times that day if it had not been Ahm who stole Lys.

Cautiously I approached the flank of the cliffs, where they terminated in an abrupt escarpment as though some all powerful hand had broken off a great section of rock and set it upon the surface of the earth. It was now quite dark, and as I crept around the edge of the cliff, I saw at a little distance a great fire around which were many figures—apparently human figures. Cautioning Nobs to silence, and he had learned many lessons in the value of obedience since we had entered Caspak, I slunk forward, taking advantage of whatever cover I could find, until from behind a bush I could distinctly see the creatures assembled by the fire. They were human and yet not human. I should say that they were a little higher in the scale of evolution than Ahm, possibly occupying a place of evolution between that of the Neanderthal man and what is known as the Grimaldi race. Their features were distinctly negroid, though their skins were white. A considerable portion of both torso and limbs were covered with short hair, and their physical proportions were in many aspects apelike, though not so much so as were Ahm's. They carried themselves in a more erect position, although their arms were considerably longer than those of the Neanderthal man. As I watched them, I saw that they possessed a language, that they had knowledge of fire and that they carried besides the wooden club of Ahm, a thing which resembled a crude stone hatchet. Evidently they were very low in the scale of humanity, but they were a step upward from those I had previously seen in Caspak.

But what interested me most was the slender figure of a dainty girl, clad only in a thin bit of muslin which scarce covered her knees—a bit of muslin torn and ragged about the lower hem. It was Lys, and she was alive and so far as I could see, unharmed. A huge brute with thick lips and prognathous jaw stood at her shoulder. He was talking loudly and gesticulating wildly. I was close enough to hear his words, which were similar to the language of Ahm, though much fuller, for there were many words I could not understand. However I caught the gist of what he was saying—which in effect was that he had found and captured this Galu, that she was his and that he defied anyone to question his right of possession. It appeared to me, as I afterward learned was the fact, that I was witnessing the most primitive of marriage ceremonies. The assembled members of the tribe looked on and listened in a sort of dull and perfunctory apathy, for the speaker was by far the mightiest of the clan.

There seemed no one to dispute his claims when he said, or rather shouted, in stentorian tones: "I am Tsa. This is my she. Who wishes her more than Tsa?"

"I do," I said in the language of Ahm, and I stepped out into the firelight before them. Lys gave a little cry of joy and started toward me, but Tsa grasped her arm and dragged her back.

"Who are you?" shrieked Tsa. "I kill! I kill! I kill!"

"The she is mine," I replied, "and I have come to claim her. I kill if you do not let her come to me." And I raised my pistol to a level with his heart. Of course the creature had no conception of the purpose of the strange little implement which I was poking toward him. With a sound that was half human and half the growl of a wild beast, he sprang toward me. I aimed at his heart and fired, and as he sprawled headlong to the ground, the others of his tribe, overcome by fright at the report of the pistol, scattered toward the cliffs— while Lys, with outstretched arms, ran toward me.

As I crushed her to me, there rose from the black night behind us and then to our right and to our left a series of frightful screams and shrieks, bellowings, roars and growls. It was the night-life of this jungle world coming into its own— the huge, carnivorous nocturnal beasts which make the nights of Caspak hideous. A shuddering sob ran through Lys' figure. "O God," she cried, "give me the strength to endure, for his sake!" I saw that she was upon the verge of a breakdown, after all that she must have passed through of fear and horror that day, and I tried to quiet and reassure her as best I might; but even to me the future looked most unpromising, for what chance of life had we against the frightful hunters of the night who even now were prowling closer to us?

Now I turned to see what had become of the tribe, and in the fitful glare of the fire I perceived that the face of the cliff was pitted with large holes into which the man-things were clambering. "Come," I said to Lys, "we must follow them. We cannot last a half-hour out here. We must find a cave." Already we could see the blazing green eyes of the hungry carnivora. I seized a brand from the fire and hurled it out into the night, and there came back an answering chorus of savage and rageful protest; but the eyes vanished for a short time. Selecting a burning branch for each of us, we advanced toward the cliffs, where we were met by angry threats.

"They will kill us," said Lys. "We may as well keep on in search of another refuge."

"They will not kill us so surely as will those others out there," I replied. "I am going to seek shelter in one of these caves; nor will the man-things prevent." And I kept on in the direction of the cliff's base. A huge creature stood upon a ledge and brandished his stone hatchet. "Come and I will kill you and take the she," he boasted.

"You saw how Tsa fared when he would have kept my she," I replied in his own tongue. "Thus will you fare and all your fellows if you do not permit us to come in peace among you out of the dangers of the night."

"Go north," he screamed. "Go north among the Galus, and we will not harm you. Some day will we be Galus; but now we are not. You do not belong among us. Go away or we will kill you. The she may remain if she is afraid, and we will keep her; but the he must depart."

"The he won't depart," I replied, and approached still nearer. Rough and narrow ledges formed by nature gave access to the upper caves. A man might scale them if unhampered and unhindered, but to clamber upward in the face of a belligerent tribe of half-men and with a girl to assist was beyond my capability.

"I do not fear you," screamed the creature. "You were close to Tsa; but I am far above you. You cannot harm me as you harmed Tsa. Go away!"

I placed a foot upon the lowest ledge and clambered upward, reaching down and pulling Lys to my side. Already I felt safer. Soon we would be out of danger of the beasts again closing in upon us. The man above us raised his stone hatchet above his head and leaped lightly down to meet us. His position above me gave him a great advantage, or at least so he probably thought, for he came with every show of confidence. I hated to do it, but there seemed no other way, and so I shot him down as I had shot down Tsa.

"You see," I cried to his fellows, "that I can kill you wherever you may be. A long way off I can kill you as well as I can kill you near by. Let us come among you in peace. I will not harm you if you do not harm us. We will take a cave high up. Speak!"

"Come, then," said one. "If you will not harm us, you may come. Take Tsa's hole, which lies above you."

The creature showed us the mouth of a black cave, but he kept at a distance while he did it, and Lys followed me as I crawled in to explore. I had matches with me, and in the light of one I found a small cavern with a flat roof and floor which followed the cleavage of the strata. Pieces of the roof had fallen at some long-distant date, as was evidenced by the depth of the filth and rubble in which they were embedded. Even a superficial examination revealed the fact that nothing had ever been attempted that might have improved the livability of the cavern; nor, should I judge, had it ever been cleaned out. With considerable difficulty I loosened some of the larger pieces of broken rock which littered the floor and placed them as a barrier before the doorway. It was too dark to do more than this. I then gave Lys a piece of dried meat, and sitting inside the entrance, we dined as must have some of our ancient forbears at the dawning of the age of man, while far below the open diapason of the savage night rose weird and horrifying to our ears. In the light of the great fire still burning we could see huge, skulking forms, and in the blacker background countless flaming eyes.

Lys shuddered, and I put my arm around her and drew her to me; and thus we sat throughout the hot night. She told me of her abduction and of the fright she had undergone, and together we thanked God that she had come through unharmed, because the great brute had dared not pause along the danger-infested way. She said that they had but just reached the cliffs when I arrived, for on several occasions her captor had been forced to take to the trees with her to escape the clutches of some hungry cave-lion or saber-toothed tiger, and that twice they had been obliged to remain for considerable periods before the beasts had retired.

Nobs, by dint of much scrambling and one or two narrow escapes from death, had managed to follow us up the cliff and was now curled between me and the doorway, having devoured a piece of the dried meat, which he seemed to relish immensely. He was the first to fall asleep; but I imagine we must have followed suit soon, for we were both tired. I had laid aside my ammunition-belt and rifle, though both were close beside me; but my pistol I kept in my lap beneath my hand. However, we were not disturbed during the night, and when I awoke, the sun was shining on the tree-tops in the distance. Lys' head had drooped to my breast, and my arm was still about her.

Shortly afterward Lys awoke, and for a moment she could not seem to comprehend her situation. She looked at me and then turned and glanced at my arm about her, and then she seemed quite suddenly to realize the scantiness of her apparel and drew away, covering her face with her palms and blushing furiously. I drew her back toward me and kissed her, and then she threw her arms about my neck and wept softly in mute surrender to the inevitable.

It was an hour later before the tribe began to stir about. We watched them from our "apartment," as Lys called it. Neither men nor women wore any sort of clothing or ornaments, and they all seemed to be about of an age; nor were there any babies or children among them. This was, to us, the strangest and most inexplicable of facts, but it recalled to us that though we had seen many of the lesser developed wild people of Caspak, we had never yet seen a child or an old man or woman.

After a while they became less suspicious of us and then quite friendly in their brutish way. They picked at the fabric of our clothing, which seemed to interest them, and examined my rifle and pistol and the ammunition in the belt around my waist. I showed them the thermos-bottle, and when I poured a little water from it, they were delighted, thinking that it was a spring which I carried about with me—a never-failing source of water supply.

One thing we both noticed among their other characteristics: they never laughed nor smiled; and then we remembered that Ahm had never done so, either. I asked them if they knew Ahm; but they said they did not.

One of them said: "Back there we may have known him." And he jerked his head to the south.

"You came from back there?" I asked. He looked at me in surprise.

"We all come from there," he said. "After a while we go there." And this time he jerked his head toward the north. "Be Galus," he concluded.

Many times now had we heard this reference to becoming Galus. Ahm had spoken of it many times. Lys and I decided that it was a sort of original religious conviction, as much a part of them as their instinct for self-preservation—a primal acceptance of a hereafter and a holier state. It was a brilliant theory, but it was all wrong. I know it now, and how far we were from guessing the wonderful, the miraculous, the gigantic truth which even yet I may only guess at—the thing that sets Caspak apart from all the rest of the world far more definitely than her isolated geographical position or her impregnable barrier of giant cliffs. If I could live to return to civilization, I should have meat for the clergy and the layman to chew upon for years—and for the evolutionists, too.

After breakfast the men set out to hunt, while the women went to a large pool of warm water covered with a green scum and filled with billions of tadpoles. They waded in to where the water was about a foot deep and lay down in the mud. They remained there from one to two hours and then returned to the cliff. While we were with them, we saw this same thing repeated every morning; but though we asked them why they did it we could get no reply which was intelligible to us. All they vouchsafed in way of explanation was the single word Ata. They tried to get Lys to go in with them and could not understand why she refused. After the first day I went hunting with the men, leaving my pistol and Nobs with Lys, but she never had to use them, for no reptile or beast ever approached the pool while the women were there—nor, so far as we know, at other times. There was no spoor of wild beast in the soft mud along the banks, and the water certainly didn't look fit to drink.

This tribe lived largely upon the smaller animals which they bowled over with their stone hatchets after making a wide circle about their quarry and driving it so that it had to pass close to one of their number. The little horses and the smaller antelope they secured in sufficient numbers to support life, and they also ate numerous varieties of fruits and vegetables. They never brought in more than sufficient food for their immediate needs; but why bother? The food problem of Caspak is not one to cause worry to her inhabitants.

The fourth day Lys told me that she thought she felt equal to attempting the return journey on the morrow, and so I set out for the hunt in high spirits, for I was anxious to return to the fort and learn if Bradley and his party had returned and what had been the result of his expedition. I also wanted to relieve their minds as to Lys and myself, as I knew that they must have already given us up for dead. It was a cloudy day, though warm, as it always is in Caspak. It seemed odd to realize that just a few miles away winter lay upon the storm-tossed ocean, and that snow might be falling all about Caprona; but no snow could ever penetrate the damp, hot atmosphere of the great crater.

We had to go quite a bit farther than usual before we could surround a little bunch of antelope, and as I was helping drive them, I saw a fine red deer a couple of hundred yards behind me. He must have been asleep in the long grass, for I saw him rise and look about him in a bewildered way, and then I raised my gun and let him have it. He dropped, and I ran forward to finish him with the long thin knife, which one of the men had given me; but just as I reached him, he staggered to his feet and ran on for another two hundred yards—when I dropped him again. Once more was this repeated before I was able to reach him and cut his throat; then I looked around for my companions, as I wanted them to come and carry the meat home; but I could see nothing of them. I called a few times and waited, but there was no response and no one came. At last I became disgusted, and cutting off all the meat that I could conveniently carry, I set off in the direction of the cliffs. I must have gone about a mile before the truth dawned upon me—I was lost, hopelessly lost.

The entire sky was still completely blotted out by dense clouds; nor was there any landmark visible by which I might have taken my bearings. I went on in the direction I thought was south but which I now imagine must have been about due north, without detecting a single familiar object. In a dense wood I suddenly stumbled upon a thing which at first filled me with hope and later with the most utter despair and dejection. It was a little mound of new-turned earth sprinkled with flowers long since withered, and at one end was a flat slab of sandstone stuck in the ground. It was a grave, and it meant for me that I had at last stumbled into a country inhabited by human beings. I would find them; they would direct me to the cliffs; perhaps they would accompany me and take us back to their abodes—to the abodes of men and women like ourselves. My hopes and my imagination ran riot in the few yards I had to cover to reach that lonely grave and stoop that I might read the rude characters scratched upon the simple headstone. This is what I read:

HERE LIES JOHN TIPPET
ENGLISHMAN KILLED BY TYRANNOSAURUS
10 SEPTEMBER A.D., 1916, R.I.P.

Tippet! It seemed incredible. Tippet lying here in this gloomy wood! Tippet dead! He had been a good man, but the personal loss was not what affected me. It was the fact that this silent grave gave evidence that Bradley had come this far upon his expedition and that he too probably was lost, for it was not our intention that he should be long gone. If I had stumbled upon the grave of one of the party, was it not within reason to believe that the bones of the others lay scattered somewhere near.

CHAPTER NINE

As I stood looking down upon that sad and lonely mound, wrapped in the most dismal of reflections and premonitions, I was suddenly seized from behind and thrown to earth. As I fell, a warm body fell on top of me, and hands grasped my arms and legs. When I could look up, I saw a number of giant fingers pinioning me down, while others stood about surveying me. Here again was a new type of man—a higher type than the primitive tribe I had just quitted. They were a taller people, too, with better-shaped skulls and more intelligent faces. There were less of the ape characteristics about their features, and less of the negroid, too. They carried weapons, stone-shod spears, stone knives, and hatchets—and they wore ornaments and breech-cloths—the former of feathers worn in their hair and the latter made of a single snake-skin cured with the head on, the head depending to their knees.

Of course I did not take in all these details upon the instant of my capture, for I was busy with other matters. Three of the warriors were sitting upon me, trying to hold me down by main strength and awkwardness, and they were having their hands full in the doing, I can tell you. I don't like to appear conceited, but I may as well admit that I am proud of my strength and the science that I have acquired and developed in the directing of it—that and my horsemanship I always have been proud of. And now, that day, all the long hours that I had put into careful study, practice and training brought me in two or three minutes a full return upon my investment. Californians, as a rule, are familiar with ju-jutsu, and I especially had made a study of it for several years, both at school and in the gym of the Los Angeles Athletic Club, while recently I had had, in my employ, a Jap who was a wonder at the art.

It took me just about thirty seconds to break the elbow of one of my assailants, trip another and send him stumbling backward among his fellows, and throw the third completely over my head in such a way that when he fell his neck was broken. In the instant that the others of the party stood in mute and inactive surprise, I unslung my rifle—which, carelessly, I had been carrying across my back; and when they charged, as I felt they would, I put a bullet in the forehead of one of them. This stopped them all temporarily—not the death of their fellow, but the report of the rifle, the first they had ever heard. Before they were ready to attack me again, one of them spoke in a commanding tone to his fellows, and in a language similar but still more comprehensive than that of the tribe to the south, as theirs was more complete than Ahm's. He commanded them to stand back and then he advanced and addressed me.

He asked me who I was, from whence I came and what my intentions were. I replied that I was a stranger in Caspak, that I was lost and that my only desire was to find my way back to my companions. He asked where they were and I told him toward the south somewhere, using the Caspakian phrase which, literally translated, means "toward the beginning." His surprise showed upon his face before he voiced it in words. "There are no Galus there," he said.

"I tell you," I said angrily, "that I am from another country, far from Caspak, far beyond the high cliffs. I do not know who the Galus may be; I have never seen them. This is the farthest north I have been. Look at me—look at my clothing and my weapons. Have you ever seen a Galu or any other creature in Caspak who possessed such things?"

He had to admit that he had not, and also that he was much interested in me, my rifle and the way I had handled his three warriors. Finally he became half convinced that I was telling him the truth and offered to aid me if I would show him how I had thrown the man over my head and also make him a present of the "bang-spear," as he called it. I refused to give him my rifle, but promised to show him the trick he wished to learn if he would guide me in the right direction. He told me that he would do so tomorrow, that it was too late today and that I might come to their village and spend the night with them. I was loath to lose so much time; but the fellow was obdurate, and so I accompanied them. The two dead men they left where they had fallen, nor gave them a second glance—thus cheap is life upon Caspak.

These people also were cave-dwellers, but their caves showed the result of a higher intelligence that brought them a step nearer to civilized man than the tribe next "toward the beginning." The interiors of their caverns were cleared of rubbish, though still far from clean, and they had pallets of dried grasses covered with the skins of leopard, lynx, and bear, while before the entrances were barriers of stone and small, rudely circular stone ovens. The walls of the cavern to which I was conducted were covered with drawings scratched upon the sandstone. There were the outlines of the giant red-deer, of mammoths, of tigers and other beasts. Here, as in the last tribe, there were no children or any old people. The men of this tribe had two names, or rather names of two syllables, and their language contained words of two syllables; whereas in the tribe of Tsa the words were all of a single syllable, with the exception of a very few like Atis and Galus. The chief's name was To-jo, and his household consisted of seven females and himself. These women were much more comely, or rather less hideous than those of Tsa's people; one of them, even, was almost pretty, being less hairy and having a rather nice skin, with high coloring.

They were all much interested in me and examined my clothing and equipment carefully, handling and feeling and smelling of each article. I learned from them that their people were known as Band-lu, or spear-men; Tsa's race was called Sto-lu—hatchet-men. Below these in the scale of evolution came the Bo-lu, or club-men, and then the Alus, who had no weapons and no language. In that word I recognized what to me seemed the most remarkable discovery I had made upon Caprona, for unless it were mere coincidence, I had come upon a word that had been handed down from the beginning of spoken language upon earth, been handed down for millions of years, perhaps, with little change. It was the sole remaining thread of the ancient woof of a dawning culture which had been woven when Caprona was a fiery mount upon a great land-mass teeming with life. It linked the unfathomable then to the eternal now. And yet it may have been pure coincidence; my better judgment tells me that it is coincidence that in Caspak the term for speechless man is Alus, and in the outer world of our own day it is Alalus.

The comely woman of whom I spoke was called So-ta, and she took such a lively interest in me that To-jo finally objected to her attentions, emphasizing his displeasure by knocking her down and kicking her into a corner of the cavern. I leaped between them while he was still kicking her, and obtaining a quick hold upon him, dragged him screaming with pain from the cave. Then I made him promise not to hurt the she again, upon pain of worse punishment. So-ta gave me a grateful look; but To-jo and the balance of his women were sullen and ominous.

Later in the evening So-ta confided to me that she was soon to leave the tribe.

"So-ta soon to be Kro-lu," she confided in a low whisper. I asked her what a Kro-lu might be, and she tried to explain, but I do not yet know if I understood her. From her gestures I deduced that the Kro-lus were a people who were armed with bows and arrows, had vessels in which to cook their food and huts of some sort in which they lived, and were accompanied by animals. It was all very fragmentary and vague, but the idea seemed to be that the Kro-lus were a more advanced people than the Band-lus. I pondered a long time upon all that I had heard, before sleep came to me. I tried to find some connection between these various races that would explain the universal hope which each of them harbored that some day they would become Galus. So-ta had given me a suggestion; but the resulting idea was so weird that I could scarce even entertain it; yet it coincided with Ahm's expressed hope, with the various steps in evolution I had noted in the several tribes I had encountered and with the range of type represented in each tribe. For example, among the Band-lu were such types as So-ta, who seemed to me to be the highest in the scale of evolution, and To-jo, who was just a shade nearer the ape, while there were others who had flatter noses, more prognathous faces and hairier bodies. The question puzzled me. Possibly in the outer world the answer to it is locked in the bosom of the Sphinx. Who knows? I do not.

Thinking the thoughts of a lunatic or a dope-fiend, I fell asleep; and when I awoke, my hands and feet were securely tied and my weapons had been taken from me. How they did it without awakening me I cannot tell you. It was humiliating, but it was true. To-jo stood above me. The early light of morning was dimly filtering into the cave.

"Tell me," he demanded, "how to throw a man over my head and break his neck, for I am going to kill you, and I wish to know this thing before you die."

Of all the ingenuous declarations I have ever heard, this one copped the proverbial bun. It struck me as so funny that, even in the face of death, I laughed. Death, I may remark here, had, however, lost much of his terror for me. I had become a disciple of Lys' fleeting philosophy of the valuelessness of human life. I realized that she was quite right—that we were but comic figures hopping from the cradle to the grave, of interest to practically no other created thing than ourselves and our few intimates.

Behind To-jo stood So-ta. She raised one hand with the palm toward me—the Caspakian equivalent of a negative shake of the head.

"Let me think about it," I parried, and To-jo said that he would wait until night. He would give me a day to think it over; then he left, and the women left—the men for the hunt, and the women, as I later learned from So-ta, for the warm pool where they immersed their bodies as did the shes of the Sto-lu. "Ata," explained So-ta, when I questioned her as to the purpose of this matutinal rite; but that was later.

I must have lain there bound and uncomfortable for two or three hours when at last So-ta entered the cave. She carried a sharp knife—mine, in fact, and with it she cut my bonds.

"Come!" she said. "So-ta will go with you back to the Galus. It is time that So-ta left the Band-lu. Together we will go to the Kro-lu, and after that the Galus. To-jo will kill you tonight. He will kill So-ta if he knows that So-ta aided you. We will go together."

"I will go with you to the Kro-lu," I replied, "but then I must return to my own people 'toward the beginning.'"

"You cannot go back," she said. "It is forbidden. They would kill you. Thus far have you come—there is no returning."

"But I must return," I insisted. "My people are there. I must return and lead them in this direction."

She insisted, and I insisted; but at last we compromised. I was to escort her as far as the country of the Kro-lu and then I was to go back after my own people and lead them north into a land where the dangers were fewer and the people less murderous. She brought me all my belongings that had been filched from me—rifle, ammunition, knife, and thermos bottle, and then hand in hand we descended the cliff and set off toward the north.

For three days we continued upon our way, until we arrived outside a village of thatched huts just at dusk. So-ta said that she would enter alone; I must not be seen if I did not intend to remain, as it was forbidden that one should return and live after having advanced this far. So she left me. She was a dear girl and a stanch and true comrade—more like a man than a woman. In her simple barbaric way she was both refined and chaste. She had been the wife of To-jo. Among the Kro-lu she would find another mate after the manner of the strange Caspakian world; but she told me very frankly that whenever I returned, she would leave her mate and come to me, as she preferred me above all others. I was becoming a ladies' man after a lifetime of bashfulness!

At the outskirts of the village I left her without even seeing the sort of people who inhabited it, and set off through the growing darkness toward the south. On the third day I made a detour westward to avoid the country of the Band-lu, as I did not care to be detained by a meeting with To-jo. On the sixth day I came to the cliffs of the Sto-lu, and my heart beat fast as I approached them, for here was Lys. Soon I would hold her tight in my arms again; soon her warm lips would merge with mine. I felt sure that she was still safe among the hatchet people, and I was already picturing the joy and the love-light in her eyes when she should see me once more as I emerged from the last clump of trees and almost ran toward the cliffs.

It was late in the morning. The women must have returned from the pool; yet as I drew near, I saw no sign of life whatever. "They have remained longer," I thought; but when I was quite close to the base of the cliffs, I saw that which dashed my hopes and my happiness to earth. Strewn along the ground were a score of mute and horrible suggestions of what had taken place during my absence— bones picked clean of flesh, the bones of manlike creatures, the bones of many of the tribe of Sto-lu; nor in any cave was there sign of life.

Closely I examined the ghastly remains fearful each instant that I should find the dainty skull that would shatter my happiness for life; but though I searched diligently, picking up every one of the twenty-odd skulls, I found none that was the skull of a creature but slightly removed from the ape. Hope, then, still lived. For another three days I searched north and south, east and west for the hatchetmen of Caspak; but never a trace of them did I find. It was raining most of the time now, and the weather was as near cold as it ever seems to get on Caprona.

At last I gave up the search and set off toward Fort Dinosaur. For a week—a week filled with the terrors and dangers of a primeval world—I pushed on in the direction I thought was south. The sun never shone; the rain scarcely ever ceased falling. The beasts I met with were fewer in number but infinitely more terrible in temper; yet I lived on until there came to me the realization that I was hopelessly lost, that a year of sunshine would not again give me my bearings; and while I was cast down by this terrifying knowledge, the knowledge that I never again could find Lys, I stumbled upon another grave—the grave of William James, with its little crude headstone and its scrawled characters

recording that he had died upon the 13th of September—
killed by a saber-tooth tiger.

I think that I almost gave up then. Never in my life have I
felt more hopeless or helpless or alone. I was lost. I could
not find my friends. I did not even know that they still lived;
in fact, I could not bring myself to believe that they did. I
was sure that Lys was dead. I wanted myself to die, and yet I
clung to life—useless and hopeless and harrowing a thing as
it had become. I clung to life because some ancient, reptilian
forbear had clung to life and transmitted to me through the
ages the most powerful motive that guided his minute
brain—the motive of self-preservation.

At last I came to the great barrier-cliffs; and after three
days of mad effort—of maniacal effort—I scaled them. I
built crude ladders; I wedged sticks in narrow fissures; I
chopped toe-holds and finger-holds with my long knife; but
at last I scaled them. Near the summit I came upon a huge
cavern. It is the abode of some mighty winged creature of
the Triassic—or rather it was. Now it is mine. I slew the
thing and took its abode. I reached the summit and looked
out upon the broad gray terrible Pacific of the far-southern
winter. It was cold up there. It is cold here today; yet here I
sit watching, watching, watching for the thing I know will
never come—for a sail.

CHAPTER TEN

Once a day I descend to the base of the cliff and hunt, and fill my stomach with water from a clear cold spring. I have three gourds which I fill with water and take back to my cave against the long nights. I have fashioned a spear and a bow and arrow, that I may conserve my ammunition, which is running low. My clothes are worn to shreds. Tomorrow I shall discard them for leopard-skins which I have tanned and sewn into a garment strong and warm. It is cold up here. I have a fire burning and I sit bent over it while I write; but I am safe here. No other living creature ventures to the chill summit of the barrier cliffs. I am safe, and I am alone with my sorrows and my remembered joys—but without hope. It is said that hope springs eternal in the human breast; but there is none in mine.

I am about done. Presently I shall fold these pages and push them into my thermos bottle. I shall cork it and screw the cap tight, and then I shall hurl it as far out into the sea as my strength will permit. The wind is off-shore; the tide is running out; perhaps it will be carried into one of those numerous ocean-currents which sweep perpetually from pole to pole and from continent to continent, to be deposited at last upon some inhabited shore. If fate is kind and this does happen, then, for God's sake, come and get me!

It was a week ago that I wrote the preceding paragraph, which I thought would end the written record of my life upon Caprona. I had paused to put a new point on my quill and stir the crude ink (which I made by crushing a black variety of berry and mixing it with water) before attaching my signature, when faintly from the valley far below came an unmistakable sound which brought me to my feet, trembling with excitement, to peer eagerly downward from my dizzy ledge. How full of meaning that sound was to me you may guess when I tell you that it was the report of a firearm! For a moment my gaze traversed the landscape beneath until it was caught and held by four figures near the base of the cliff—a human figure held at bay by three hyaenodons, those ferocious and blood-thirsty wild dogs of the Eocene. A fourth beast lay dead or dying near by.

I couldn't be sure, looking down from above as I was; but yet I trembled like a leaf in the intuitive belief that it was Lys, and my judgment served to confirm my wild desire, for whoever it was carried only a pistol, and thus had Lys been armed. The first wave of sudden joy which surged through me was short-lived in the face of the swift-following conviction that the one who fought below was already doomed. Luck and only luck it must have been which had permitted that first shot to lay low one of the savage creatures, for even such a heavy weapon as my pistol is entirely inadequate against even the lesser carnivora of Caspak. In a moment the three would charge! A futile shot would but tend more greatly to enrage the one it chanced to hit; and then the three would drag down the little human figure and tear it to pieces.

And maybe it was Lys! My heart stood still at the thought, but mind and muscle responded to the quick decision I was forced to make. There was but a single hope—a single chance—and I took it. I raised my rifle to my shoulder and took careful aim. It was a long shot, a dangerous shot, for unless one is accustomed to it, shooting from a considerable altitude is most deceptive work. There is, though, something about marksmanship which is quite beyond all scientific laws.

Upon no other theory can I explain my marksmanship of that moment. Three times my rifle spoke—three quick, short syllables of death. I did not take conscious aim; and yet at each report a beast crumpled in its tracks!

From my ledge to the base of the cliff is a matter of several thousand feet of dangerous climbing; yet I venture to say that the first ape from whose loins my line has descended never could have equaled the speed with which I literally dropped down the face of that rugged escarpment. The last two hundred feet is over a steep incline of loose rubble to the valley bottom, and I had just reached the top of this when there arose to my ears an agonized cry— "Bowen! Bowen! Quick, my love, quick!"

I had been too much occupied with the dangers of the descent to glance down toward the valley; but that cry which told me that it was indeed Lys, and that she was again in danger, brought my eyes quickly upon her in time to see a hairy, burly brute seize her and start off at a run toward the near-by wood. From rock to rock, chamoislike, I leaped downward toward the valley, in pursuit of Lys and her hideous abductor.

He was heavier than I by many pounds, and so weighted by the burden he carried that I easily overtook him; and at last he turned, snarling, to face me. It was Kho of the tribe of Tsa, the hatchet-men. He recognized me, and with a low growl he threw Lys aside and came for me. "The she is mine," he cried. "I kill! I kill!"

I had had to discard my rifle before I commenced the rapid descent of the cliff, so that now I was armed only with a hunting knife, and this I whipped from its scabbard as Kho leaped toward me. He was a mighty beast, mightily muscled, and the urge that has made males fight since the dawn of life on earth filled him with the blood-lust and the thirst to slay; but not one whit less did it fill me with the same primal passions. Two abysmal beasts sprang at each other's throats that day beneath the shadow of earth's oldest cliffs—the man of now and the man-thing of the earliest, forgotten then, imbued by the same deathless passion that has come down unchanged through all the epochs, periods and eras of time from the beginning, and which shall continue to the incalculable end—woman, the imperishable Alpha and Omega of life.

Kho closed and sought my jugular with his teeth. He seemed to forget the hatchet dangling by its aurochs-hide thong at his hip, as I forgot, for the moment, the dagger in my hand. And I doubt not but that Kho would easily have bested me in an encounter of that sort had not Lys' voice awakened within my momentarily reverted brain the skill and cunning of reasoning man.

"Bowen!" she cried. "Your knife! Your knife!"

It was enough. It recalled me from the forgotten eon to which my brain had flown and left me once again a modern man battling with a clumsy, unskilled brute. No longer did my jaws snap at the hairy throat before me; but instead my knife sought and found a space between two ribs over the savage heart. Kho voiced a single horrid scream, stiffened spasmodically and sank to the earth. And Lys threw herself into my arms. All the fears and sorrows of the past were wiped away, and once again I was the happiest of men.

With some misgivings I shortly afterward cast my eyes upward toward the precarious ledge which ran before my cave, for it seemed to me quite beyond all reason to expect a dainty modern belle to essay the perils of that frightful climb. I asked her if she thought she could brave the ascent, and she laughed gayly in my face.

"Watch!" she cried, and ran eagerly toward the base of the cliff. Like a squirrel she clambered swiftly aloft, so that I was forced to exert myself to keep pace with her. At first she frightened me; but presently I was aware that she was quite as safe here as was I. When we finally came to my ledge and I again held her in my arms, she recalled to my mind that for several weeks she had been living the life of a cave-girl with the tribe of hatchet-men. They had been driven from their former caves by another tribe which had slain many and carried off quite half the females, and the new cliffs to which they had flown had proven far higher and more precipitous, so that she had become, through necessity, a most practiced climber.

She told me of Kho's desire for her, since all his females had been stolen and of how her life had been a constant nightmare of terror as she sought by night and by day to elude the great brute. For a time Nobs had been all the protection she required; but one day he disappeared—nor has she seen him since. She believes that he was deliberately made away with; and so do I, for we both are sure that he never would have deserted her. With her means of protection gone, Lys was now at the mercy of the hatchet-man; nor was it many hours before he had caught her at the base of the cliff and seized her; but as he bore her triumphantly aloft toward his cave, she had managed to break loose and escape him.

"For three days he has pursued me," she said, "through this horrible world. How I have passed through in safety I cannot guess, nor how I have always managed to outdistance him; yet I have done it, until just as you discovered me. Fate was kind to us, Bowen."

I nodded my head in assent and crushed her to me. And then we talked and planned as I cooked antelope-steaks over my fire, and we came to the conclusion that there was no hope of rescue, that she and I were doomed to live and die upon Caprona. Well, it might be worse! I would rather live here always with Lys than to live elsewhere without her; and she, dear girl, says the same of me; but I am afraid of this life for her. It is a hard, fierce, dangerous life, and I shall pray always that we shall be rescued from it—for her sake.

That night the clouds broke, and the moon shone down upon our little ledge; and there, hand in hand, we turned our faces toward heaven and plighted our troth beneath the eyes of God. No human agency could have married us more sacredly than we are wed. We are man and wife, and we are content. If God wills it, we shall live out our lives here. If He wills otherwise, then this manuscript which I shall now consign to the inscrutable forces of the sea shall fall into friendly hands. However, we are each without hope. And so we say good-bye in this, our last message to the world beyond the barrier cliffs.

(Signed) Bowen J. Tyler, Jr. Lys La R. Tyler.

THE END